OUTLAWS

OUTLAWS

Kenneth Ulyatt

Illustrated with contemporary material

J. B. Lippincott Company

Philadelphia and New York

The photographs in this book have been taken from famous American collections. They are all very old. The original negatives in many cases have been lost and copies taken from old prints. That is why they are spotted, faded, and sometimes torn. But I have left them unretouched so that you know you are looking at the real thing.

Nearly all the paintings were done by W. H. D. Koerner (1878–1938), who traveled the old trails and painted the western scene well over fifty years ago. There are also works by Charles Marion Russell and Karl Bodmer. Some of the sketches, like those of the flatboat and the Lawrence massacre, were drawn by people who were there at the time.

The publishers and I would like to thank the following for their kind permission to reproduce the photographs, paintings, and drawings that appear in this book:

Arizona Historical Society, page 103; The Bettmann Archive, Inc., pages 40 and 122; Connecticut State Library Museum, Hartford, Connecticut, page 36; Mary Evans Picture Library, page 48; The Thomas Gilcrease Institute of American History and Art, Tulsa, Oklahoma, page 20; Great Falls *Tribune*, Great Falls, Montana, page 85; Illinois State Historical Library, page 33; Kansas State Historical Society, pages 24–25, 27, 72–73, 95, 96–97, and 101; Library of Congress, back of jacket and pages 5, 44, 63, and 65; Missouri Historical Society, page 16; National Archives, pages 64 and 89; Rare Book Division, The New York Public Library–Astor, Lenox, and Tilden Foundation, pages 12–13; Oklahoma Historical Society, pages 81 and 82; Ruth Koerner Oliver, title page and pages 54, 56–57, 68, 92–93, 105, and 120; Wells Fargo Bank History Room, San Francisco, California, page 6; Western History Collections, University of Oklahoma Library, pages 59, 61, 87, 103, 113, and 125.

U.S. Library of Congress Cataloging in Publication Data

Ulyatt, Kenneth, birth date
  Outlaws.

  Includes index.
  1. The West—History—Juvenile literature. 2. Outlaws—United States—History—Juvenile literature. I. Title.
F591.U4 1978   364.1'5'0978   77-10127   ISBN-0-397-31773-5

Contents

Joe Brown

*Robbed Shasta Stage
in 1877 with Dave Dye and
Sam Brown*

"Throw down the box!"

The order came from the figure in the middle of the road. His hat was pulled low over his eyes; a neckerchief masked the lower part of his face. He stood with his legs wide apart, the butt of a Winchester carbine pulled tight into his shoulder. The black bore of the barrel looked unwaveringly at the driver of the coach.

The red Concord was still rocking on its thoroughbraces from the sudden stop, and the telltale plume of dust that had followed the coach as it rolled through the golden California hills drifted slowly down. It cloaked the heaving flanks of the nervous horses, the passengers huddled on the roof.

For just a second the driver hesitated and the guard at his side cautiously moved a cramped leg. Instantly, the masked man swung the carbine in a small arc and the guard changed his mind about reaching for the shotgun. He pushed his hands higher, as if to touch the bright blue sky. Again came the command: "Throw down the box!" and from the bushes at the side of the trail another masked figure stepped into view. On the slope above, behind the halted stage, a third man made his presence known.

Hastily, the driver bent down and fumbled between his knees, pulling the treasure box from beneath his seat. He lifted it by the worn leather handles and tipped it over the edge of the leather boot. It fell to the ground with a crash that startled the offside wheeler and the horse jumped forward, pushing into the pair ahead. Involuntarily the driver caught up the reins of the six-horse team, which he had dropped when he'd raised his hands.

The masked man with the Winchester stepped aside and nodded to his companion, who ran toward the lead horse.

"Right, get goin'—and don't stop till you reach town." They needed no second bidding. The lead horse took a stinging blow on the rump. The driver slammed the long brake forward and with a crash the Wells Fargo stage jerked into motion, rocking the passengers violently in their seats. A gun roared as one bandit put a shot over their heads. White faces looked back . . . and then they were gone, the rising dust climbing once again behind them as they clattered down the trail. Briefly the bandits watched and then, when they were sure that the frightened driver was continuing on his way, they turned their attention to the green box in the road and prepared to break it open with an axe.

Did Joe Brown smile as he pulled down his mask and set to work? For he was the man who had stopped the stage. He looks serious enough in the photograph that's stuck into Chief Detective Hume's "black book" of bandits who robbed Wells Fargo during those golden days when the company's coaches were bringing the bullion down from the mines in the mountains. But the photograph was taken on a serious occasion—when Joe Brown was being welcomed to the state prison.

On that bright day when he stopped the Shasta stage, Joe held the whole world at gunpoint. It was his one claim to a dubious sort of fame. It was the day he was going to get rich, the day he'd show the whole world who was boss. We don't know what his thoughts were that day. We don't know what plans he had to spend the money. All we really know about Joe Brown is that, with his companions Dave Tye and Tom Brown, he was caught. And with the photograph in Chief Detective Hume's book his day of fame ended. He's now forgotten, just a strangely haunting picture in a book that you and a few other people will look at for a moment and dismiss. Most of the badmen who plagued the West didn't even get that!

Some, of course, gained a more enduring fame in songs and stories that make them out to be heroes: Billy the Kid, the James brothers, Wes Hardin, and the like. The truth is different: a little sordid, a little sad.

The Terrible Harpes

They called it the Wilderness Road. It led up through the Great Smoky Mountains and down along the Wautaga River. One branch turned north toward the Cumberland Gap and Kentucky, the other curved west and south into Tennessee.

Daniel Boone had blazed the first trail in the 1760s. He was one of the Long Hunters, men so called because they stayed a long time in the wilderness, hunting deer. The skin of a buck could be sold for a dollar —"buck" soon became the slang word for dollar—and a band of determined hunters could bring back a thousand skins in one season.

When Boone first came over the mountains from the eastern colonies and dropped down into the great forest wilderness, he found it crisscrossed with buffalo paths and with two old Indian trails: the Warrior Path, by which Cherokee war parties went north in search of their enemies; and the Chickasaw Trace, which ran southwest down to the old French trading town of Natchez. Boone was interested in opening up the rich land between the mountains and the Mississippi, the bluegrass land of Kentucky and the new territories of western Tennessee. The pioneers followed Boone's Trace by the thousands, proud and fearless men with their wives and families, seeking land to clear and to farm and make their own. They hammered out the Wilderness Road until it was a wide track snaking through the virgin forest. And they pushed the trees back, and they cleared their patches, and they built their farms—and they built frontier towns like Knoxville.

Knoxville was the gateway to the still unknown West, a roaring, lawless town on the south branch of the Wilderness Road. It was crowded with buckskinned hunters and blanket-clad Indians and the wagons of the pioneers heading west. And in addition to the stores and stables and

9

legitimate businesses that lined the streets, there were saloons and gambling rooms.

For other men had come west with the pioneers. Disgruntled soldiers, disappointed farmers, the footloose and adventurous and the men with dark secrets . . . "desperadoes fleeing justice, suspected or convicted felons escaped from the grasp of the law, the horse thief, the counterfeiter, and the robber." It was a pattern we shall see again and again as the frontier moves west.

Among these wild visitors to Knoxville were the terrible Harpes. They came, originally, from North Carolina, where their father had fought on the side of the British during the Revolutionary War. There were two of them: Micajah, or "Big" Harpe; and Wiley, "Little" Harpe. They were in their late twenties, bearded, robust men, surly in countenance and with short, thick black hair.

They fled from North Carolina after the Revolution and made their way to Tennessee, taking two sisters, Susan and Betsy Roberts, with them. For two years they lived with a wandering band of Cherokee Indians—outlaws like themselves, hunted by both red men and white. During these years they learned the forest lessons of concealment and quiet movement that were to stand them in such good stead. They dressed in the buckskin of the frontiersman—the women as well as the men—and they carried muskets and tomahawks, with spears in their belts. But the Harpes wore no hats, a peculiar trait that was to single them out from their coonskin-capped countrymen in the bloody times to come.

In the spring of 1797 the Harpes parted from their Indian friends and took the Wilderness Road to Knoxville. On that lonely road they committed their first known crime. They stopped a young preacher riding between the settlements. They turned out his pockets, searched the pages of his Bible for hidden money, and left him unarmed and on foot in the forest. It was a mean crime, but one to which they left a strange and deliberate clue. Before they disappeared into the wilderness, they looked back at him and shouted—like madmen, the preacher later said —"We are the Harpes!" Then they vanished as suddenly as they had come. It was the only crime they committed that did not end in murder.

Knoxville suited the Harpes. They cleared a patch along a creek to the west of the town and settled down, seemingly as honest farmers. They began to raise hogs for the town butcher. And then, suddenly, there was an outbreak of petty thievery among the little farms, and the Harpes appeared in town with more pork and more money than honest farmers could possibly possess. Things culminated in a raid on Tiel's stables in the town, and a hastily raised posse trailed the stolen horses to the Harpes' patch on Beaver Creek. It was deserted, but they had left a trail that anyone could follow. Stupidly, without any attempt to cover their tracks, the Harpes had driven the horses into the mountains, and there on the road the posse caught them, alone and hatless.

They offered no resistance. Sullenly they surrendered, appearing meekly to submit to their capture. It was only on the march back to town that the old madness flared up. "We are the Harpes!" With a bound, they broke free from their captors and plunged into the trees. The posse crashed after them, but with the cunning of Indians the two men had vanished.

In vain the posse retraced their steps and started again. In vain Tiel urged the men on in their search. After hours of going around in circles the tired posse gave up, and, as the light failed, they turned once more toward home.

The trees beside the trail stood thick and silent. No movement disturbed the thickets as the shadows lengthened. Only a growing, menacing darkness spread along the Wilderness Road—a darkness that was to last, apart from brief splashes of violent light, for nearly two years.

Later that night, two hatless figures loomed in the doorway of an inn on the banks of the Holston River a few miles away. It was a rowdy, evil place kept by a man named Hughes. Staying the night at that "grog-shop" was a pioneer called Johnson. His body was found two days later floating in the river. He had been savagely knifed and disemboweled, and gravel had been pushed into his belly in an unsuccessful attempt to make the body sink.

And, once more, the Harpes had disappeared.

11

Next, a peddler was found on the road. He had been tomahawked and a few items of women's clothing had been stolen from his pack. A little further westward, a few days later, two more bodies were discovered on the trail, shot and tomahawked. More clothing had been stolen. The Wilderness Road was becoming a place to avoid if you traveled alone.

In December of that year, a young man named Stephen Langford arrived at John Pharris's inn, just beyond the settlement of Little Rock Castle. A thirty-mile stretch of unbroken forest hemmed the road to the next settlement. On the door of his tavern, the innkeeper had tacked a notice advising travelers to band together before continuing their journey. One by one, the pioneers added their names to a list and waited until a party large enough to travel in safety had gathered.

On the day Langford reached the inn, however, there were no other travelers waiting, and Pharris counseled him to stay overnight. In the morning, looking back up the road he had already traveled and hoping

for someone to arrive so that he could start westward once more, Langford was pleased to see a small group approaching. There were a big man and a smaller one, both hatless, and two ragged women. Their few possessions were slung over the backs of two horses that they drove before them, Indian style.

Langford was anxious to press on, and rough company was better than no company at all on that dangerous trail. He bought them breakfast and suggested traveling together. The strangers said little, but they watched Langford put on his greatcoat and stuff his wallet into his pocket after paying the innkeeper. Then they walked down the trail with him and disappeared into the wilderness. A week later Langford's body was found—stripped, robbed, and tomahawked.

The Harpes had now notched up five murders and, as had previously happened, the wild spell of violence was followed by apathy and carelessness. A posse found them sitting on a log beside the road. They wore fine linen shirts and one had a greatcoat. In their possession was found a wallet with the name "Stephen Langford" inside. They were taken to the nearest township and thrown into jail.

As news of the capture of the terrible Harpes spread, people from all

"The Wilderness Road"
by Karl Bodmer.

over the settlements came to look at them behind bars. "We are the Harpes!" Big Harpe grew boastful under the constant attention, offering to fight any two men in the crowd, with his freedom as the prize. John Biegler, the jailer, was worried about his charges, as the entries in his account book show. Early February: "12 shillings for two horse locks to chain the men's feet to the ground, 3 pence for one bolt." And, as one of the women was pregnant: "1 shilling and 10 pence for tea" and "1 shilling and 6 pence for sugar for the ladies." (Robert M. Coates, *The Outlaw Years* [London: The Macauley Co., 1930].)

A few days later there is the sum of eighteen shillings, paid to the midwife who delivered Susan Harpe of a daughter in the jail.

And then, on March 16, 1798, the last entry of the whole affair: "12 shillings for mending the wall in the jail where the prisoners escaped." (Coates, *The Outlaw Years.*)

Violence flared again along the Wilderness Road. The son of an old Indian fighter, Colonel Trabue, was shot and tomahawked for a sack of beans and a bushel of flour. The news of two more murders in the northwest indicated that the Harpes were moving through Kentucky toward the Ohio River. And at last the whole country was roused into action.

Descriptions of the murderous band were posted along the Road. The state of Kentucky offered "a reward of THREE HUNDRED DOLLARS to any person who shall apprehend and deliver into the custody of the jailer of the Danville District the said MICAIAH HARP, and a like reward for apprehending and delivering as aforesaid the said WILEY HARP, to be paid out of the Public Treasury." In the haste even the names were misspelled!

Then the settlers organized themselves into bands called "Regulators" and took the law into their own hands. Hughes's tavern was burned down, together with any other evil place where it was suspected the Harpes might have taken refuge. Other thieves were rounded up. "Judge Lynch and Squire Birch" ruled the land; and when the Regulators had finished, fifteen men had been hanged, hundreds flogged, and hundreds more driven west. But the Harpes were still at large.

14

The Pirates of Cave-in-Rock

Although thousands of pioneers followed Boone's Trace through the wilderness in their wagons, there was another route to the West—by flatboat. Flatboats were rafts thirty or forty feet long, with boarded sides and sometimes a cabin in the middle as a shelter. There were two long oars or "sweeps" on each side for steering. The hopeful pioneer loaded his family and belongings aboard at the head of the waterway, probably just below Pittsburgh, and then pushed off, trusting to the Ohio River's broad stream to carry him west to the settlements. It was a hazardous trip. Boats snagged on rocks and submerged tree trunks or were overturned in treacherous rapids. Indians kept pace with the travelers to ambush them when they put ashore. Worse still, pirates lay in wait at Hurricane Bars.

About five hundred miles down the Ohio from Pittsburgh, the flatboats passed the mouth of the Wabash River. From then on, until they reached the Cumberland River, they sailed through the most dangerous stretch of their journey. Islands and sandbars split the gliding surface of the river; swinging currents tossed the boats toward the shoals called Hurricane Bars. And there, on the banks of the Ohio, in a deep limestone cave, was the lair of the pirates and boat-wreckers . . . men like "Innkeeper" Wilson and "Colonel Plug" and his lieutenant, "Nine Eyes."

The pirates kept watch from the bank. If the worried pioneers put in to ask about the passage through the Bars, the pirates fell on them ruthlessly. If a flatboat risked the run on its own and snagged on the sand, "Innkeeper" Wilson's men would rush to the rescue. Only what they rescued would be the goods on board; the luckless pioneer family were left to drown!

"Colonel Plug" had earned his name by the trick of hiding aboard a flatboat upriver and boring into the caulking between the logs as it came down to the Bars. When the boat began to founder, "Colonel Plug" would wave his followers to the "rescue."

In the early summer of 1798, Cave-in-Rock was swarming with outlaws driven west by the great hunt of the Regulators. And to Cave-in-Rock, at last, came the two Harpes, to rendezvous with the women from whom they had been separated ever since the escape from jail.

In this lawless community, killing was a necessary part of robbery. The

A broadhorn flatboat, so called from the long steering sweeps on each side.

pioneer had already left his home far behind him and relatives would not expect to hear news for as much as several years. Killing the victim brought no reprisals; it also prevented him from warning other travelers of the ambush. So the Harpes' ferocity was at first welcomed among the outlaws. But the madness that had prompted their earlier crimes now burst forth in a frenzy of killing and torture that sickened even the pirates. It came to a climax with the massacre of two families from a flatboat, lured ashore one afternoon. Over their campfires that night, the pirates were sorting out the booty when a wild cry rang out from the dark cliff behind them. They turned, startled.

A horse tottered on the very edge of the bluff and, pale against the night sky, the naked figure of one of the flatboat victims waved wildly down at them. Then the horse was lashed from behind, leaped out from the clifftop, and crashed onto the rocks below. The Harpes now came, roaring with laughter, from the shadows. They had concealed the body of the pioneer that afternoon, carried it up the cliff in the dark, and, strapping it on the back of the horse, had put on this savage show for their friends.

It was too much, even for the badmen. The Harpes and their women were driven from Cave-in-Rock, outlawed even by the outlaws! They went back into the wilderness from which they had come. That year they killed heaven knows how many people. They saw a horse that they liked; they killed the owner. They wanted a rifle; they killed again, and took one. Five men were axed in one bloody raid alone. They moved back and forth through the woods, baffling their pursuers. And with sinister cunning they now joined the chase for themselves. "We're huntin' the Harpes," they would cry to any band they met, thus explaining their ragged clothes and their vast armory. And the unsuspecting strangers would relax and put down their guns—only to have these wild men turn upon them suddenly with tomahawks and knives. But retribution was following close on their trail.

Old Colonel Trabue, whose son they had killed for a sack of beans, was a justice of the peace, and, methodically, he drew up a list of the Harpes' victims and made out an affidavit to their known crimes. He had their descriptions printed and circulated among the settlements. Other determined men began to take up the hunt—skilled trappers and posses with hunting dogs. Gradually, the settlers plucked up courage and began to watch out for the wild-eyed pair with black hair and beards. With a bit of luck, when they next came out of hiding the people would be prepared.

Late in July, 1799, the Harpes appeared for the last time. They had acquired new, black clothes from somewhere and passed themselves off as Methodist preachers. On the trail from Red Bank to Nashville they called at the cabin of James Tompkins, who invited the pair to share his midday meal, but marveled that two preachers should be so heavily armed. "With such dreadful men as the Harpes abroad, my friend, it behooves us all to protect ourselves," was the reply. And when Tompkins innocently remarked that he was low on gunpowder, Big Harpe pulled out his own powder horn and generously poured out a cupful.

With many "Amens" and blessings the Harpes departed, laughing, no doubt, at the success of their deceit. It was to be a jest that turned against the makers. For when evening came, James Tompkins poured Harpe's powder into his own powder horn and loaded his rifle—just in case!

That night the Harpes stopped at the cabin of Moses Steigal. Mrs. Steigal admitted the men, still dressed as preachers, and introduced them to Major Love, a surveyor, who was staying the night, awaiting Steigal's return. They sat around awhile, Mrs. Steigal sewing and the men talking. Love commented upon the terrible crimes of the Harpes, and then the three men climbed to the loft to sleep.

Mrs. Steigal was still at her sewing when a noise startled her. The two preachers were climbing down from the loft, and from the blood on their hands and the mad light in their eyes she knew that something terrible had happened. "He snored too much," growled Big Harpe. "What do ye mean by putting us in with a man that snored so?"

Riding down the trail later, Moses Steigal found his cabin ablaze and his neighbors gathered around. His wife and baby were dead; Surveyor Love was somewhere in the burning house. And two more corpses further down the road pointed the way the Harpes had gone. With mounting fury Steigal gathered a posse—among them Samuel Leiper, John Williams, and James Tompkins. They rode through the night and the next day. They camped and rode on again, and on the second day of the hunt overtook their quarry.

Even at that moment the Harpes and their women were still at their deadly work; they had stopped a young man with intent to rob him. As the posse came over the hill, they scattered. Wiley ran into the thickets and disappeared, the women shrank to one side, and Big Harpe spurred his horse on down the Wilderness Road, over one hill and down into a valley. At the top of the second hill the hunters had closed to shooting range. Leiper, in the lead, fired and missed. He was still galloping, fumbling with the old muzzle-loader, when Tompkins came alongside and held out the rifle loaded with Harpe's own powder. "You're a better shot than I," he cried. "Take it." Leiper fired. Big Harpe lurched in the saddle and his horse ran off the trail. They found him in a tangle of bushes, dazed but still wielding his tomahawk. They disarmed him and waited for the rest of the posse to come up.

Leiper's shot had taken Big Harpe in the spine. He was unable to move and weakening fast. But he could still talk. For a while they could not understand what he said; then he began to speak about his murders. He expressed no regrets—except for Susan's baby, which he had "slung by the heels against a tree" when it had cried. That he did regret. But Steigal, with the picture of his own wife and baby still fresh in his mind, was not satisfied. He drew a knife and waved it before the dark face. "I'm going to cut off your head with that." He sawed at Big Harpe's neck and the criminal's dying words were still full of defiance. "You're a god-damned rough butcher, but cut on and be damned!" They put the head in a bag and set off for home.

At a crossing on the trail called Robertson's Lick, Steigal wedged Big Harpe's head in the fork of a tree and nailed it there. The skull rotted and whitened, grinning down for many a year at the travelers on the Wilderness Road.

On the old maps the spot is still marked "Harpeshead."

So the two years of terror ended. The exact number of people who

"Frontiersman" by William Cary.

met their deaths at the hands of the Harpes will never be known. There are records for thirty-nine; but there were probably many more, slain in various raids, whose bodies were never found in that primitive country.

The three-hundred-dollar reward was shared among the members of the posse, Samuel Leiper receiving a larger share (one hundred dollars) because he had felled the outlaw. No trace could be found of Wiley Harpe, but the posse took Susan and Betsy Roberts with them on their gruesome journey back to town and eventually the two women were brought to trial.

Steigal, a violent man, his thirst for vengeance still unappeased, gathered a group of friends together and rode to the court, vowing to kill the women if they were acquitted. But the charges were vague. The Harpes were the murderers. Susan's baby had been one of the victims; and at the trial it was clearly shown that the sisters had been nowhere near Steigal's cabin when the last killings had been done.

So Susanna Harpe and Betsy Roberts, as they were charged, were freed; and the sheriff, a tough old pioneer named Major William Stewart, hid them until Steigal's anger had cooled and his friends had dispersed.

In fact, both women outlived their pursuer, for he was killed in a quarrel near Cave-in-Rock a few years later. Susan drifted from town to town along the Mississippi. Betsy, the prettier of the two, found a man who was prepared to forget the past and married him. She lived quietly and industriously for the rest of her life. Women, after all, were in short supply in the wilderness.

The frontier—that vague line that separates civilization from savagery—was moving westward across the Appalachian Mountains and pushing toward the Mississippi River. The wilderness, the land between the mountains and the river, was an empty land for the moment, for no one counted the Indians who had lived there for centuries. They were going to be pushed out, anyway. It was a land only partially explored; a land that, for a long period, would be without law and order. Beyond the frontier there was always a refuge for the lawbreaker fleeing from punishment.

The Harpes were the first to plague this wilderness, and many others followed. There was Sam Mason, an honorable man turned highwayman. He terrorized the Mississippi until a bearded stranger named John Setton volunteered to go out and bring him in. Setton himself was a suspicious character and when, after many strange adventures, he eventually brought back Mason's head in a ball of clay, he was recognized as Wiley Harpe!

Then there was Joseph Hare, who specialized in holding up the coaches of the Natchez Trace. And James Ford, who combined the duties of a ferryman with those of a justice of the peace, and who was secretly the chief of a bandit gang. But the boldest and most flamboyant of them all was John Murrel, who organized hundreds of lone criminals into one huge outlaw clan and who planned to rouse the Negro slaves of the South to revolt and march on New Orleans!

And with slavery we come to the long struggle between the states that finally flared into the Civil War.

The Border Wars

There had been slavery all over colonial America, but as the country developed it gradually died out in the North. This was because the northern states took nearly all the immigrants arriving from Europe, men seeking a new life and freedom to live it as they pleased. To them, the very idea of slavery was hateful. Besides, there were so many immigrants, all busy building new cities and creating new industries, that there was really no need for slavery.

In the South it was different. The whole way of life in the southern states was based on cotton. And to tend the fields and pick the crops the southerners needed four million slaves.

All the differences that had grown up between the North and the South could have been settled peacefully—except for the issue of slavery! By the time the wilderness between the Appalachians and the Mississippi had been conquered and settled, America was divided. The states above a line drawn roughly east to west across the middle of the country permitted no slaves in their territory. Those below the line, the cotton-growing states, were slave states. It was a compromise, and like most compromises it stored up trouble for the future. For as the frontier moved across the Mississippi, a question arose concerning the new states in the West: Should they become slave states, or free?

Missouri was a slave state. On its western border was the new territory of Kansas. Under the compromise agreement the settlers themselves would decide whether they wanted slaves or not. Those who came from the North were determined to make Kansas "free soil." The settlers from the South were equally determined to bring slavery with them to the new land. The "free soil" northerners quickly tried to pass a law forming the new state and ruling out slavery. Missouri sent over bands of "border ruffians" to seize the "free soil" town of Lawrence; the northern settlers, who were also called Jayhawkers, struck back. Very soon, open warfare raged along the whole of the Kansas–Missouri border. There were honorable men fighting on both sides, convinced that their cause was the right one. But ruffians of all kinds were also drawn to the territory. Murder, robbery, and blind hatred became commonplace. All through the Civil War and for a long time afterward, "Bleeding Kansas," as it was called, was the breeding ground for some of the worst outlaws of the West.

"A Kansas Guerrilla Raid on a Slavers' Settlement" by S. J. Reader.

Quantrill's Raiders

Into Kansas, in the midst of all the troubles, rode a young man of twenty. Opinions differ about his appearance, but all agree on two things: the neatness of his clothes and the strange, secretive look of his heavy-lidded eyes. He was the son of a respectable schoolteacher in Ohio and he had been a teacher himself on occasion. He had crossed the prairies with the wagon trains of a freighting company, and he had gambled in the gold camps of the Rocky Mountains. He was also a thief, suspected of murder.

His name in Kansas was "Charley Hart" and in the "free soil" town of Lawrence he called himself an abolitionist, joining the ranks of the northerners who had vowed to abolish slavery. These men had organized an underground railroad, a route along which slaves could be spirited away from the southern plantations to freedom in the North. The southern planters paid handsomely to get their slaves back and so, secretly, Charley Hart went into business.

He rounded up freed slaves and drove them back over the border into Missouri. There, under his real name, William Clarke Quantrill, he sold them back into slavery. On the side, he indulged in a little horse-stealing as well. By 1860, Quantrill was a confirmed border bandit.

His double life came to an end in December of that year. Riding as "Charley Hart" with a party of Kansas Jayhawkers bent on liberating slaves and collecting a little booty in the process, he stopped near the plantation of a man named Morgan Walker. Now Quantrill knew Walker and was, in fact, courting his daughter, Anne. On some pretext he left the Jayhawkers and went secretly to the Walker house.

The next day, when the Jayhawkers arrived to demand the freedom of the slaves, they rode straight into an ambush. A volley of shots from the

William C. Quantrill.

The burning of Lawrence, Kansas. A sketch made a few hours after the raid by Sherman Enderton.

old harness house alongside the road cut the column to pieces; and when the shattered Jayhawkers finally got away, Quantrill's double role had been exposed and he was left firmly on the side of the Missourians.

He still continued to operate across the border, however, and, riding through Kansas in April, 1861, he was recognized, arrested, and flung into jail in Paola to await trial for his treachery in the Walker ambush. But the townspeople of Lawrence were not going to wait for the long process of the law to convict "Charley Hart." They wanted Quantrill's blood and they wanted it quickly. A posse, which was really a lynching party, set off for Paola with the intention of breaking into the jail and hanging Quantrill from the nearest tree.

The outlaw still had a few friends in Kansas, however, and Judge Thomas Hodges of the Paola Court ordered his release just as the Lawrence posse reached town. A saddled horse was waiting outside the courtroom. Under the noses of the mob, Quantrill leaped into the saddle and spurred for the Missouri border. A few days after his escape, the Civil War began. It was to last for four horrible years, but it proved to be Quantrill's golden opportunity.

Divided by the quarrel over slavery, the United States split into two nations. The southern states left the Union and banded together to form the Confederacy. Caught between the two opposing armies, Missouri found that it was impossible to stay neutral. The Union troops marched south across the state and the Confederate forces tried to stop them.

Quantrill served briefly, but bravely, with the Confederate cavalry at the battle of Wilson's Creek. But when the southern forces finally retreated into Arkansas, he turned his horse's head north and rode into history!

In western Missouri, far behind the Union lines, he gathered a band of men together. They were mostly country boys, used to guns and horses. Nevertheless, Quantrill, acting the Confederate officer, made each man practice until he was an expert shot and first-class rider. He taught them how to evade capture and live off the country. But, above all, he showed them how the new Colt revolvers could be their most effective weapon. Very soon, his strong personality, his ability to organize, and his power of command welded the band into a tight-knit, hard-hitting force—Quantrill's Raiders.

Spies were sent out to watch the Union troops and report on where their camps were situated. The lines of communication between each camp were carefully plotted. Then the raiders struck! They shot sentries, ambushed wagons and burned them; they raided the lonely outposts and massacred the men there. Riding like the wind, shooting with deadly accuracy, they would hit their chosen target without warning and then scatter into open country so as to make pursuit useless. At some secret and prearranged rendezvous point they would meet up again to plan their next raid.

Had it stopped there, Quantrill's name might have been remembered as that of the leader of the first mounted guerrillas. Like Lawrence of Arabia, he took his country's fight deep into enemy-held territory and created havoc with a small force of irregular soldiers. But the raiding had brought Quantrill's men a great deal of plunder: cash from the Union pay wagons, goods from the raided depots. And there was always the chance, as we shall see, to even some old scores.

With Missouri under martial law, the quarrels that had raged for so long on the Kansas–Missouri border could now be carried on under the pretense of war. Small bands of guerrilla fighters sprang up under both flags. And in the burning and robbery and pillaging that followed it was difficult to tell patriot from outlaw.

From Kansas came Charles Jennison and Jim Lane, bloodthirsty men both, who led the Jayhawkers into Missouri on raids that owed more to piracy than to acts of war. And under the Confederate flag rode Quantrill and George Todd and Bloody Bill Anderson. With such men in command it was no wonder that the guerrilla fighting grew more and more ruthless. No longer were the raiders fighting for the Union or the Confederate cause; they were killing, looting, and burning indiscriminately. For years afterward, the blackened brick chimney that was left standing when a log house burned down was called a "Jennison's Monument" throughout Missouri. So bad had the situation become in April, 1862, that General Totton, the officer commanding the Union forces, outlawed Quantrill and his followers. In future, said Special Order No. 47, the Union would refuse to recognize the guerrillas as regular soldiers and would shoot or hang them on sight.

Quantrill, in an attempt to gain the support of the Confederate command in Virginia, made a secret journey through the fighting lines to Richmond, the Confederate capital, to ask for a colonel's commission. But the Secretary for War refused to support the guerrillas. He told Quantrill that his men were acting like barbarians, and coldly dismissed him. Quantrill went back to Missouri seething with rage. He had been outlawed by the Union. Now he was being dismissed by the Confederacy. There was only one thing to do, he said, and that was to "raise the black flag." This meant that the outlaws, too, would give no quarter. From now on they would simply kill anyone who got in their way.

The Lawrence Massacre

The Civil War now entered its second year. The Confederacy had mounted a great offensive in the autumn of 1862, and for a moment it had seemed that the southern states might snatch victory from the North. But as the year turned, the tide of the southern effort began to ebb and the Union forces were poised to strike down the Mississippi and cut the Confederacy in two.

In Missouri, Quantrill burned with ambition for some great deed that would win approval in the Confederacy's eyes and perhaps gain him the rank of colonel. Gradually, a plan formed in his mind, and, in July, 1863, he called his men together for a council of war. The idea was simple. All the plunder that the Union had taken from Missouri during the first year of war, so he said, was stored in one small town just over the border in Kansas, the town from which the Jayhawkers had so often set out on raids before the Civil War had begun. If they struck quickly, he assured them, and with the same tactics that had brought them such success elsewhere, they would get as much money in that one town as they could find anywhere else in Kansas.

With a yell of approval, the men voted for the raid. His heavy-lidded eyes gleaming, Quantrill immediately set about planning the attack on the town whose citizens had so nearly lynched him two years before— the old "free soil" stronghold of Lawrence. Greed and revenge were marching hand in hand!

By August 18 he was ready, mounted at the head of a column of 448 men. He was "a fine figure on horseback . . . a soft black hat with a yellow or gold cord for a band, cavalry boots, a shirt ornamented with fine needlework. . . ." This was the way a farmer who saw the column pass described him. (Paul I. Wellman, *A Dynasty of Western Outlaws* [London:

31

Museum Press Ltd., 1961].) His men were less neat—unshaven, crouched over their mounts, all in low-crowned, broad-brimmed hats, wearing red flannel shirts, and armed to the teeth. At that moment Quantrill's Raiders were a disciplined force to be reckoned with.

Somewhere in those jogging, passing ranks were two young men whom we will meet again—a sandy-haired youth of twenty and a big six-footer of nineteen. Frank James and Cole Younger were setting out to learn the wartime lessons they would put to such deadly practice when peace finally came.

Quantrill marched his column for two days, dodging the Union scouts and creeping closer and closer to his objective. By the night of August 20 he had crossed the border and was looking for a road through the creeks and gullies of eastern Kansas. A farmer was roused from his bed and taken along as a guide. When Quantrill became suspicious of the man, he had him shot. Another guide was procured—and treated in the same way. Then, as they drew nearer, the ground became familiar and at last, in silence save for the thud of hooves and the creak of saddle leather, the raiders rode up to the crest of a hill and looked down at Lawrence.

There was a brief conference. Some of the men had lists of people they wanted to kill. Quantrill had marked the leaders of the Jayhawkers—in particular, Jim Lane.

The men drew their revolvers. At a signal from Quantrill they went into a trot, spreading out across the grassy slope. Then a pistol shot rang out, and with one thundering roar the riders swept down on the sleeping town.

Jim Lane was awakened by the first shouts of alarm. Without waiting to dress he ran for the fields, caught an old horse, and made for safety, leaving his wife and family to face the guerrillas. They set fire to the house and with the roar of the flames the massacre of Lawrence really began.

People came stumbling from their beds to see what was happening. The raiders shot at anyone who appeared. More buildings were set on fire. In the growing confusion the murder lists were forgotten and an orgy of killing began. Husbands were shot before their horrified wives; children were thrown aside; boys were cut down as they ran to help their fathers.

By now, looting had begun; houses were searched for money and jewelry. The liquor store was broken into and many men became drunk. People were thrown back into burning buildings to die. For four terrible hours it went on, with Quantrill calmly supervising the operation as if he were a military commander on the battlefield. Some people, it is true, he spared—among them the governor of the town—but when the raid-

A bummer, drawn
by a Yankee soldier.

ers finally withdrew, 142 Kansans lay dead under the smoke-stained sky. Quantrill had had his revenge. Lawrence was gutted and the raiders moved off with their plunder.

They left a legacy of hatred that was to fester for a long time after the Civil War was over. The massacre provoked the Union forces to drastic action. The ease with which the guerrillas had been able to live off the land suggested that they had many friends among the civilian population. Missouri, after all, had been a slave state, and, had it not been overrun by northern troops, probably would have joined the Confederacy eventually. Missourians, argued Union commander General Thomas Ewing, were southern sympathizers. Clear them out of the border counties and the guerrillas would have nowhere to go for food and shelter.

On August 25, 1863, he issued the infamous Order No. 11. Its purpose was to remove everybody from the four border counties of western Missouri. Families were given fifteen days to pack and go. There was no time to sell anything; their grain had been confiscated for the Union army; their fields were already burning. Loading what furniture and possessions they could into a wagon, driving perhaps a cow before them for milk, the farmers of Missouri left the homes they had carved out of the wilderness.

"It was a tragic hour," wrote a fourteen-year-old boy, William Wallace. "All our horses broke to work except two had been taken. . . . We had three or four yoke of oxen. Many of our neighbors had no conveyance of any kind. . . ." (Wellman, *A Dynasty of Western Outlaws.*) Out of the ten thousand inhabitants of Cass County only a few hundred were allowed to stay in the garrison towns. And, as the land emptied, Jim Lane led his Jayhawkers in from Kansas and laid the whole area to waste.

Yet the order failed to stop the Confederate guerrillas. A year later they were back, living among the deserted farms, riding the overgrown roads, and fighting the Union army with undiminished ferocity. That autumn, Bloody Bill Anderson led a force of 225 guerrillas into Centralia, about thirty miles north of the Missouri River. They pillaged the town and then, on its outskirts, stopped a train of the Wabash, St. Louis & Pacific Railroad.

They broke into the express car and took three thousand dollars in small packets. Then they turned their attention to the passengers. There were twenty-five Union soldiers traveling on the train—not as guards, but simply moving to their units. The guerrillas lined them up against the cars and one by one, in cold blood, shot them.

Frank James was in that column in Centralia, and with him was a blue-eyed, reckless lad of seventeen whom the others called "Dingus." His face was smooth, oval, and almost girlish. But there was nothing girlish about his behavior that day. He killed eight men. He was Frank's brother, and his real name was Jesse Woodson James.

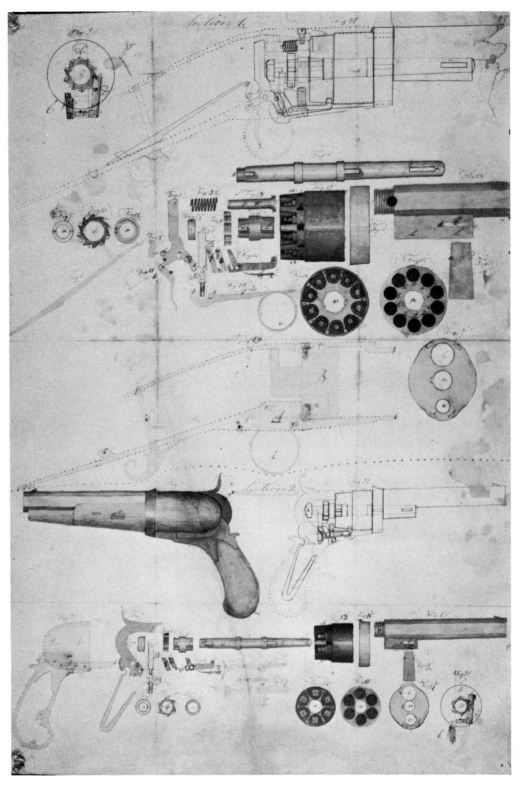

Plans for Colt handguns.

The Civil War was over.

Quantrill was dead, shot in the pelting rain near Bloomfield, Kentucky, by a band of Union guerrillas led by a deserter no better than himself.

Jim Lane was dead from a pistol ball fired by his own hand in a mood of dark depression.

Bloody Bill Anderson was dead, cut down in an ambush by a Union detachment.

And many others died too as the guerrilla columns split up into smaller gangs and feuded among themselves. For the end of the war did not bring peace to the border.

Ex-guerrillas still hunted and chased each other through Kentucky, killing and stealing. And a decision that pushed these wild riders still further along the road to outlawry was the refusal to grant the Missouri guerrillas amnesty when the war was over. If they did go home, they went as outlaws, not honorably, as returning soldiers. But many of them still went back—back to the counties cleared by Order No. 11, back to the "Burnt District," where they found ruined farms, a cemetery of "Jennison's Monuments," and a poverty-stricken, despairing population.

They stayed around for a while, dodging the victorious Union forces, yarning among themselves about the raids in which they had taken part, looking for something to do after the excitements of the war. They were all young men, in their early twenties, and in Clay County they gathered at the home of an ex-guerrilla as young and as restless as themselves—a man who had been Quantrill's most able pupil.

Sam Colt's "Equalizer"

The rifles and handguns that Daniel Boone and his pioneers carried along the Wilderness Road were all muzzle-loaders. Powder and shot had to be pushed down the barrels and rammed tight with long rods. A flint provided the spark that ignited the powder and fired the gun. Preparation for shooting was a long and cumbersome business. With the rifles carried by the soldiers during the Civil War, there were eleven things to do before the rifle was ready to fire—and three shots a minute was considered fast going!

In 1830, however, a young man named Samuel Colt had made a wooden model of a handgun that was very different from anything seen before. It had a cylinder in which there were several chambers. Colt's idea was that the cylinder revolved each time the gun was fired, bringing a fresh charge of powder and ball into line with the barrel and enabling a man to get off several shots with only one loading. Originally, he drew his plans for a gun with ten chambers in the cylinder; later, he changed this to six so that the chambers could hold a larger ball.

During the Civil War thousands of these Colt revolvers were manufactured, and men like Quantrill were quick to appreciate their many advantages. The "cap and ball" pistol, as it was often called, was still a bit of a do-it-yourself weapon all the same. The old method of ramrodding a charge down the barrel of the gun had long since gone, but the single-action Colt Navy .36 of 1851 still needed quite a bit of preparation before it was ready to fire. The gun was loaded at the front of the revolving cylinder. A measure of powder had to be poured into the chamber from a powder flask; a ball—or bullet—went in next, followed by a piece of wadding. All this was rammed home tight by operating the lever under the gun's barrel. (See Figure 1.)

Next, a percussion cap, a small metal cup shaped rather like a top hat but about the size of a pea and filled with fulminate of mercury or potassium chlorate, had to be pushed onto the nipple at the back of the chamber. Five chambers were loaded in this way; the sixth was generally left empty with the hammer resting on it as a safety precaution. Finally, a blob of grease was pushed into each chamber to prevent a stray spark from setting them all off at once! (See Figure 2.)

When the gun was cocked—by thumbing the hammer back to its full extent—the cylinder revolved and brought a loaded chamber into line with the barrel. (See Figure 3.) The gun could then be aimed with the hammer resting in its cocked position. A slight pull on the trigger and the hammer fell, the pin striking the percussion cap. This exploded to

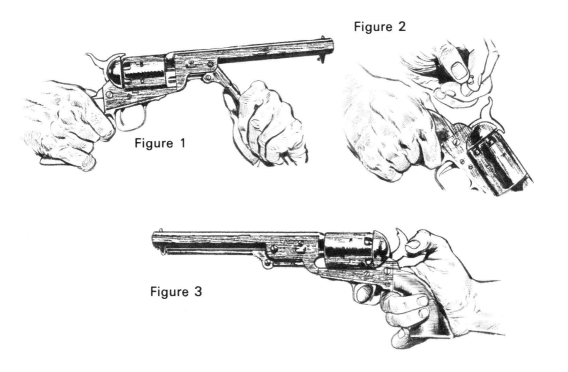

Figure 2

Figure 1

Figure 3

send a spurt of flame through the hole in the nipple, igniting the powder and driving the ball out of the gun.

The next refinement was the production of a "combustible envelope cartridge." This was a paper tube that contained the powder and ball in one package. The gunman still had to use a separate percussion cap, but the paper cartridge did away with the powder flask and separate ball and speeded loading just a bit more.

"Cap and ball" pistols had seen their day by the time Colt's famous "Peacemaker" model came into production in 1873. This gun was adopted by the army as the standard sidearm and became immensely popular all over the West. It incorporated the ultimate refinement of the revolver—the use of the metallic cartridge.

Ball, powder, and the percussion compound were now incorporated in one metallic shell, which was pushed into the cylinder *from the back,* thus avoiding the need for ramming and speeding loading even more.

Sam Colt with one of his pistols.

A soft metal rim on the shell expanded when the gun was fired, sealing the end of the chamber and making sure that the flame went out down the barrel of the gun and not back at the man holding it!

The "Peacemaker," like Jesse James's Smith & Wesson Schoefield .45 (shown on page 65), was still a single-action gun, however. That is, the hammer had to be drawn back with the thumb to cock the gun. This separate action turned the cylinder and brought a loaded chamber around into position. A touch of the trigger then released the hammer.

The final modification on the western handgun was the introduction of the "double-action" mechanism. With this type of gun, pulling the trigger did *two* things: it turned the cylinder and cocked the hammer at the same time . . . and by continuing the pull, the gunman made the hammer fall, and the gun fired.

Many inventors and dozens of patents contributed to the development of the "six-shooter." But Colt's name is the most famous and the "Peacemaker," the reliable old Model P, without any doubt at all was the most popular gun of the Old West. It had the power to bring down an opponent or a wild animal in one shot. It was accurate. And it was ruggedly built: you could use it as a club, drop it in the sand, see it kicked along by a horse—and it would still be ready for action when you picked it up and thumbed the hammer back!

In the picture on page 40, Sam Colt holds one of his celebrated pistols. They were given many imaginative names: Colt's Patent Pacifier, the Six-gun, the Hog Leg—or simply the Difference. Perhaps "Equalizer" was the most apt, for, as westerners often said, "God did not make men equal, Colonel Colt did."

The James-Younger Gang

At the end of the war, Jesse James and five other guerrillas had ridden toward Lexington, Missouri, under a white flag to surrender to the Union forces. On their way they encountered the advance party of a column of Kansas militia, who immediately opened fire. Jesse's horse was killed in the first salvo and Jesse himself took a bullet in the chest.

As the rest of the militia galloped up, the guerrillas scattered. In the confusion Jesse managed to crawl into the woods, where he lay for three days until he was discovered, weak and delirious, by a local farmer. When the wounded guerrilla was eventually brought into town, the marshal of Lexington evidently thought that the boy would die, for he did not bother to parole him but simply issued a pass that allowed Jesse to return to his family.

Months later, thin and pale but with his wound healed, the ex-guerrilla was kicking up his heels around the run-down family farm just outside the little hamlet of Kearney. His brother, Frank, had surrendered and had been paroled. Brooding over the past, listening to the boring talk of neighbors as they strove to rebuild farms destroyed by the war—it must have been a bleak time for the two young men after the heady excitement of the years with Quantrill.

Soon the pair began to ride over to Liberty, a town situated about nine miles away on a branch of the Hannibal & St. Joseph Railroad running out from Kansas City. There, they met old friends: Jim and Cole Younger, Wood and Clarence Hite, Clell Miller and Charlie Pitts, all ex-guerrillas like themselves. The little group had another thing in common—already they were tired of peace and the dull prospects of a working life on the ravaged farms. With Jesse as their leader, and in complete secrecy, they began to make plans to renew the old excitement.

Now, much has been written to show that mistreatment of the southerners by the victorious North was the direct cause of the outlawry that plagued Missouri for the next decade. Story and song paint Jesse James as an American Robin Hood, robbing the conquerors of his native state and helping the poor and starving. To be sure, there were impoverished farmers trying hard to get loans from tight-fisted banks who were not beyond laughing maliciously when those banks were robbed. And because the outlaws seemed to stand for the lost Confederate cause, gallant and defiant, they could always count on food and shelter when the need arose.

But the real truth is this: Despite the legends, there is not one shred of evidence to suggest that the James gang ever gave one cent of the proceeds of their robberies to the struggling poor of Missouri. The ex-guerrillas took up arms again not for revenge but for money. And the people they terrorized or killed on their raids were nearly all southerners like themselves.

The first target of the James–Younger gang was the Clay County Savings and Loan Association, a bank in the very town in which they had been meeting.

At about eight o'clock on a cold, blustery February morning in 1866, ten men galloped purposefully into Liberty. They all wore mufflers against the cold and long blue soldiers' overcoats with revolvers strapped prominently outside. The little cavalcade swept into the square and reined up. Three men dismounted and went quickly into the small bank, while two others waited with the horses. The remaining riders spurred around the square with revolvers drawn, "keeping things quiet."

Inside the bank, the cashier, a man with the unusual name of Greenup Bird, and his son, William, had just begun their day's work. They glanced up as the doors swung open—and found that they were looking into the black bores of leveled revolvers! Two of the men leaped over the counter as the startled cashier rose from his stool. Greenup Bird couldn't believe what was obviously happening. Banks, in those days, were regarded with awe throughout the farming community; no one

Cole	Jesse	Bob	Frank
Younger	James	Younger	James
		(rear)	

The James boys and the Younger brothers.

would dream of robbing them like this, in broad daylight. But there was no awe in the raiders' manner. "Make a move and we'll shoot," warned one man, pushing William Bird toward the vault. "Damn you, be quick and open up."

Inside the vault he produced an old grain sack and the dazed William Bird swept gold and silver coins from the shelves into its open mouth. Meanwhile, a second robber was helping himself to notes, stamps, and bonds from a large tin box on the counter.

When he had taken all he could find, he prodded Greenup Bird toward the vault, and father and son were shut inside. Just before the door slammed the leader of the gang made a grim pun. "Stay in there," he shouted. "Don't you know all Birds should be caged?" But there was no humor in the manner of the gang's getaway; it had all the hallmarks of getaways made by Quantrill's Raiders. The robbers ran out of the bank, hitched the bulging sacks to their saddle horns, and then mounted. Whooping and shooting into the air, the ten blue-coated riders milled about in the square while the shopkeepers and residents crouched behind their doors. The war had taught them to keep out of the way when a wild bunch "hurrahed" the town.

The gang moved off. As they went up the street a young student, George Wymore, was hurrying to his lessons. Seeing the riders thundering toward him, he turned and ran back toward his house. One of the bunch wheeled and leveled his revolver. Four shots rang out and the youth fell to the frozen ground, killed instantly. The townsfolk found out afterward that any one of the bullets would have proved fatal—a tribute to the rider's deadly marksmanship!

The thunder of hooves died away up the road toward Excelsior Springs and, as people approached the sprawled body of the young boy, Greenup Bird and his son burst out of the vault to tell their story.

A posse trailed the riders for some way out of town, but the blizzard that had been threatening since dawn now swept over Missouri. Long before, however, the wild raiders had scattered. The gang's first bank robbery was over.

There was one very obvious fact about the Liberty raid that gives a clue to the gang's success and tells us why they were able to operate for so many years without capture. The riders were muffled against the cold but they did not wear masks. They knew the town and the people. Had they not called Cashier Bird by name? And, in turn, some of the townspeople must have known the raiders. But it was the old story of the guerrilla raids all over again. Keep quiet, offer no resistance, and you might just escape. Open your mouth and, like young Wymore, you could end up with four bullets in your back.

Jesse James and Cole Younger went south to Texas to exchange the gold pieces for silver and notes with a man they knew in San Antonio from their guerrilla days. They couldn't spend that kind of money in Missouri without arousing suspicion. Returning home, they lay low for eight months. Jesse was supposed to be recovering from his war wound; Frank James was at his books. Then, in October, they struck at the bank in Lexington—and got clean away with two thousand dollars! This became the pattern of their operations. Carefully spying out the land beforehand, they would mount a surprise and often vicious attack on their target, "hurrahing" the townspeople into hiding during the raid. Then away into the countryside to share the loot and trickle back inconspicuously to their homes, where, once more, they would lie low, spend the proceeds of the robbery, and plan the next raid.

For nearly five years, Jesse and Frank James continued to live at the farm in Kearney, suspected of being concerned with the robberies, certainly, but always able to provide alibis when the pursuit came too close. For there were now men on their trail. When ex-guerrillas struck at the bank in Savannah, the townspeople were not all cowed into submission. Led by their judge, they fought back and drove the bandits off, empty-handed. When Jesse and his "boys" rode into Richmond in May of the following year, yelling their fearsome "hurrahs" and firing their revolvers, the citizens there fought back, too. Three men and two children were killed in the Richmond affair, and by now the countryside was thoroughly aroused. Posses tracked down three of the robbers and strung them up to the nearest tree without ceremony.

But the raids still went on: at Russellville, in Kentucky; at Gallatin, in

Missouri—where Jesse coldly shot the cashier in the head, claiming that he was a Union officer and an enemy of the guerrillas; at Corydon in Iowa; and at the Kansas City Fair Ground. Stagecoaches, too, were ambushed and the passengers robbed. Then in 1874 came the first of a series of spectacular holdups that were to carry the James boys' names around the world—Missouri's first really spectacular train robbery.

In 1810 there were no railways in the United States. By 1830 a mere thirty-two miles of track existed. But by the time the Civil War broke out, the railway boom had begun. Dozens of companies had been formed and some thirty thousand miles of track were in use. Soon the rails were being pushed out onto the prairie, and by 1868 the continent was linked by steel. The Union Pacific, building from the east through Nebraska and Wyoming, and the Central Pacific, coming from the West Coast and snaking through the Rocky Mountains, joined up in Utah, at Promontory. A symbolic golden spike was driven in to secure the last rail.

The railroads presented the wild riders of Missouri with a golden opportunity for yet more outlawry. By 1874 Jesse James and his gang had become notorious. Gone was the old secrecy; the gang rode openly under Jesse's ruthless leadership. Arrogantly they posed with their rifles and revolvers for a studio portrait (see page 44); they even took a photographer to one of their mountain hideouts, confident that they could take on anybody the law sent against them and still evade capture.

They were not the first outlaws to think of robbing trains. In Indiana in the same year that the James gang rode into Liberty, four brothers named Reno stopped a train of the Ohio & Mississippi Railroad and robbed the express car—the locked and guarded car that was usually hauled behind the engine and carried money and other valuable freight. Breaking into the car, the Reno brothers stole ten thousand dollars. And Jesse's gang had derailed a train on the Rock Island line near Council Bluffs in Iowa in 1873; but that was a wrecking reminiscent of the ruthless plundering the guerrillas had carried out under Bill Anderson at Centralia. This time Jesse was planning something more spectacular!

Gad's Hill was a tiny hamlet in southern Missouri named after Charles Dickens' country house in England. There were few buildings—only

about fifteen people lived there—but the village did boast a railway station. This was a simple wooden platform alongside the track of the Iron Mountain Railroad. Trains rolling down from St. Louis and bound for Little Rock in Arkansas had to be flagged down by the railroad agent if they were to stop.

One day in January, 1874, five men rode into Gad's Hill. Their long blue overcoats flapped around their cavalry leggings; their holstered revolvers bounced on their hips. They all wore white hoods with holes cut in them for eyes and mouth, and they quickly took the railroad agent prisoner and proceeded to round up the entire population. Herding their prisoners around a fire near the station—it was bitterly cold—the gang filled in the time waiting for the train by robbing the storekeeper of seven hundred dollars and taking his rifle. Then they hoisted a red flag on a pole and threw the points lever for a branch line that ran off the main track toward an old sawmill.

Train No. 7, the Little Rock Express, was running late that day. Swaying behind the engine and tender were two coaches and a sleeper with twenty-five passengers aboard, and a combined mail, baggage, and express car, in which the gang were particularly interested. As the train approached Gad's Hill late in the afternoon, the engineer saw the red flag fluttering in the winter wind and reached for the brake. The guard, seeing the fire and the crowd of people and thinking that something was wrong with the track, swung down from his car. As he did so he was surprised to see the engine veer off onto the branch line. He was even more surprised when two hooded men stepped up to him with leveled revolvers. "We've been waiting for you for some time," said one. "Stand still or I'll blow your head off."

His companions stepped forward and threw the points lever again to prevent the train from reversing back onto the main line. Two more of the robbers leaped up into the cab and pushed the engineer and fireman off the footplate. Herding the crew of the train together and leaving one man on guard, the rest of the gang ran down the line of coaches, banging

Railroad bandits—a newspaper drawing of 1905.

on the sides of them with their gun butts and shouting at the passengers, who were beginning to stick their heads out the windows to see what was happening.

"Get your head back or you'll lose it!" threatened one hooded figure, waving a double-barreled shotgun. In the express car, the messenger had drawn a loaded pistol, but resolution failed him when two of the gang covered him simultaneously and advised him to "Lay that pistol down, gently." Taking the key, the robbers opened the safe and began to pull out packages of money, stuffing them into the pockets of their faded overcoats. When they had finished, one of them asked the messenger for the receipt book and a pencil. Opening the book, he scrawled across the page these words: "Robbed at Gad's Hill."

The gang then went through the passenger coaches with a grain sack, demanding money and valuables. There was no resistance, for the passengers guessed, despite the white hoods, that they were face to face with the James gang. But for once there was to be no killing. The robbers seemed to be in a high good humor; one of them exchanged hats with a passenger; another asked a minister in the coach to pray for them. When the loot was all tucked away they shook hands with the engineer and advised him to "Always stop when you see the red flag." Still covering the townspeople and the train with their revolvers, they mounted up and began to back their horses slowly away from the tracks.

Suddenly their leader spurred forward, pulled a sheet of paper from his pocket, and thrust it toward the startled passengers. "Give that to the editor of the St. Louis *Dispatch,*" commanded Jesse James. There was complete silence as a man leaned down and took the paper. Then with a yell Jesse whipped up his horse and the gang streamed away.

The sheet of paper, which the astonished passengers began to read as the gang galloped away, contained Jesse's own account of the raid. The description of the robbers was deliberately wrong and a space had been left for the total amount of money stolen.

The southbound train on the Iron Mountain Railroad was boarded here this evening by five heavily armed men, and robbed of ——— dollars. The robbers arrived at the station a few minutes before the arrival of the train and arrested the station agent and put him under guard, then threw the train on the switch. The robbers were all large men, none of them under six feet tall. They were all masked, and started in a southerly direction after they had robbed the express. . . . They were all mounted on fine, blooded horses. There is a hell of an excitement in this part of the country. (*The English Westerner's Brand Book,* vol. 16, no. 2 [January 1974].)

The last sentence in this audacious report was almost an understatement. For by now the James–Younger gang was news all over America. Safe in the big towns and the eastern states, the bulk of the population was eager to read about the bandits of the "Wild West." And the newspapers obliged with long accounts of the gang's deeds and much speculation when facts were few and far between. A romantic aura began to surround the leaders of this vicious crew. "Missouri's Bold Rovers," one newspaper called them. And trading on this publicity, a mere three months after the Gad's Hill robbery, Jesse rode boldly into Kansas City in the finest clothes money could buy to marry his childhood sweetheart, Zerelda Mimms.

But the activities of the outlaws were really far from romantic. In sixteen years they raided a dozen banks, held up four stagecoaches, and robbed seven trains. These were the crimes they were *known* to have committed; many more were attributed to them. In these forays they killed ten men; eleven, if you include Jack Rafferty, the engineer of the wrecked Rock Island Express, who was scalded to death in the crash. And the people they wounded and injured—the bank employees, detectives, and innocent citizens—were beyond counting.

For the first ten years of their operations, the gang lived a charmed life. A few members were killed or captured but this did not matter; there were always plenty of young recruits from among whom the leaders could take their pick. But the original group of ex-guerrillas and relatives who had come together at Liberty did not change, and this loyalty undoubtedly contributed to the gang's success.

The last year of this decade of outlawry was marked by two successful robberies. In May, the gang held up the stage between San Antonio and Austin, Texas, and got away with three thousand dollars. By July, they had moved back to Missouri and stopped the Kansas City–St. Louis Flyer at Otterville by piling railroad ties on the track and setting fire to them. The holdup followed the usual pattern: the gang terrorized the crew and broke open the safe in the express car. Then they went through the train with leveled revolvers, holding out a sack into which the cowed passengers dropped their money and valuables. The haul was fifteen thousand dollars.

With them on the Otterville raid was a persuasive Minnesotan named Bill Chadwell. And it was Chadwell who talked the gang into a grand tour of his native state, a trip through the country of wooded hills and lakes where the deer were plentiful—but more important, where the country banks were unprepared for robbery!

They went north by train, eight of them: Jesse and Frank and the three Youngers, Cole, Jim, and Bob; Clell Miller and Charlie Pitts, both veterans of Quantrill's guerrilla band; and the enthusiastic Bill Chadwell. They were well dressed and looked prosperous. They visited St. Paul and Minneapolis and then bought horses and rode south in twos and threes so as not to attract attention. En route, they wore linen "dusters," the long coats of farmers and stock buyers. And they pretended to be cattle buyers out looking for choice stock. Their target was the First National Bank in Mankato, but a chance meeting pushed Mankato from the pages of history. As they rode into the town a man hailed Jesse from the sidewalk. Jesse shook his head. "Man, I don't know you," he said, and rode on. From that moment there was the possibility of the news going around that the James gang was in town.

Camping in the woods several miles out of Mankato, they talked it over, and then Bill Chadwell suggested that they have a go at Northfield, fifty miles to the east. It was a prosperous little town, he explained, with one bank, the First National, in which the entire county kept its money. The James and Younger boys listened—and then made the worst decision in their outlaw lives. They mounted up next morning and rode for Northfield.

The town drowsed in the autumn sun as Bill Chadwell and Cole Younger rode in to reconnoiter. They crossed a small iron bridge over the Cannon River, which divided the town in two, and drew rein in the small square beyond. They looked around.

On the right-hand side of the square were two buildings, a small one that housed the town's two hardware stores (owned by J. A. Allen and A. E. Manning), and then, separated from the hardware stores by a narrow alley, the big stone Scriver building. This was a two-story block with imposing arched windows, and it stretched down to the far corner of the square. Around the corner of the Scriver block, in Division Street, an iron staircase ran up the outside of the building to the offices on the second floor. Beyond the staircase was the entrance to the First National Bank. Its offices ran back through the Scriver block to a small door opening onto the narrow alley. Facing the bank, on the other side of Division Street, was Wheeler & Blackman's drugstore and, next to it, a small hotel, The Dampier House. All were to play an important part in what happened the next day.

The two bandits moved casually around, noting the buildings and the roads in and out of the town. Then, evidently satisfied, they rode back to the outlaws' camp to report. That night, Jesse picked the men for the "inside" work and divided the rest into two parties that would "hurrah" the town. From the sleepy look of things that afternoon there wouldn't be much trouble. Bill Chadwell was at pains to paint the Northfield citizens as slow-witted country folk. The gang were cocky and confident. After the raid they would cut the telegraph wires to make pursuit more difficult.

September 7, 1876, looked as if it was going to be just another day for the inhabitants of Northfield. Upstream, the flour mill was working full blast. In the First National Bank, Joe Heywood, the cashier, was talking to his two tellers, Frank Wilcox and A. E. Bunker. Manning and Allen were busy in their respective stores. Over on Division Street, Henry Wheeler, a young medical student home on vacation, was helping his father in the drugstore. There were other citizens about, too—Nicholas Gustavson, a Norwegian immigrant who didn't understand much English, and a man named Elias Stacey. These were just some of the people who were going to prove Bill Chadwell very wrong in his opinions of country folk.

Just before noon, three men clad in linen dusters clattered across the iron bridge and dismounted before the Scriver block. Tethering their horses, they asked about a good place to eat. The church clock up on

"Dividing the Loot" by W. H. D. Koerner.

the hill was chiming twelve as they walked into Jeft's Restaurant and ordered a meal. They didn't take off their dusters, for they were pretty heavily armed underneath. But they aroused no suspicion, and shortly before one o'clock they strolled back to the square and sat on some packing cases in front of Manning's hardware store.

Then the church clock struck one and, leisurely, the three men got up and strolled to the corner of the Scriver block. For a moment they inspected their horses. That moment, as the echoes of the bell died away, was the last moment of peace Northfield was to know for some time. From over the river came a sudden outburst of noise—the staccato crack of six-guns, the screaming of guerrilla yells. Over the bridge and into the square thundered Bob Younger, Bill Chadwell, and Clell Miller, linen dusters flapping in the wind, hats pulled low and revolvers blazing.

At the same moment, Cole and Jim Younger swept into the square from the other side, Cole swinging down from his horse in the middle of Division Street. With a pistol in each hand, he began shooting, and, at the same time, Jesse, Frank, and Charlie Pitts, the "inside men," ran from the horses they had been inspecting and burst through the doors of the bank.

All around the square, people were running for cover as the bandits raced up and down, raising the dust and shouting orders. Gustavson, who couldn't understand what was being said, tried to cross the street. Cole Younger felled him with one bullet. For those first few moments it looked as if the old "hurrahing" tactics were going to succeed again. But the Minnesotans lived deep in deer country; they were hunters, and many of them were veterans of the Civil War. They were not going to be cowed that easily. Almost immediately the movement to strike back at the bandits began.

From the drugstore opposite the bank, young Henry Wheeler saw the three men run in with drawn revolvers and knew that the bank was being robbed. There were no guns in the drugstore, but he remembered that in the hotel next door was a Sharps carbine. Ignoring the ricocheting bullets and the shouting outlaws, he made a dash for the doors of The

"Outlaws" by W. H. D. Koerner.

Dampier House, grabbed the gun and some ammunition from its case, and raced upstairs to a front window.

In the hardware stores, Manning and Allen had unlocked their gun racks and were loading everything that came to hand and yelling for men to come and get the guns. Elias Stacey seized the first gun he could get hold of and raced up to the second floor of the Scriver block. What he carried was a shotgun and loads of "bird shot"; with it, he was about to hit nearly every man in the gang.

Cole had remounted and was thundering up and down Division Street with the rest of them. Dust and powder smoke rose in the afternoon sunlight. The crash of glass was added to the noise as windows began to go. When young Wheeler appeared at the upstairs window of The Dampier House with the Sharps carbine, Clell Miller spun his horse and

took a quick shot at him. Wheeler calmly leveled the carbine and knocked Miller out of the saddle.

From the top of the iron staircase on the opposite side of the street, Stacey began to blast away with his shotgun. The pellets were not lethal but they hurt. Bill Chadwell was half blinded by a burst and two of the Youngers were hit.

Now Manning decided to take a hand. Stepping out of his store, he ran along the front of the Scriver building with a loaded rifle in his hands. Cole Younger saw him and turned to charge. Manning straightened and coolly put a bullet through the bandit's shoulder. Still Cole came on. At that moment, a shot from Wheeler's carbine took Cole's hat off and the outlaw lurched around and disappeared into the dust of Division Street. Bill Chadwell came weaving drunkenly into the square, his face bloodied by Stacey's bird shot. Manning brought him down with a bullet through his chest.

Inside the bank things were not going well either. Heywood had refused to open the inner door of the vault and had been pistol-whipped by Charlie Pitts; he lay senseless and bleeding on the floor. Bunker had made a dash for the back door, hit it with his shoulder, and burst through. As he ran out of the alley, Jim Younger came out of the melee in Division Street and hit him with a snap shot. Nevertheless, Bunker crawled to the safety of the hardware building.

By now, the "inside men" could hear the rifles booming above the six-guns in the street. Leaving the vault, they scooped up money from the tills and stuffed it into their pockets. As they made for the door Jesse turned and saw Heywood pulling himself up by gripping the counter. The outlaw chief shot the cashier in the head, killing him instantly. At that moment Cole rode up to the bank doors and yelled: "Come on! They're killing us out here!"

There was shooting on all sides now as Jesse stepped into the street and took in the scene. Clell Miller and Bill Chadwell lay dead in the dirt. Bob Younger's horse was down and Bob himself crouched under the iron staircase, trying to fire effectively with his left hand because his right hung uselessly at his side. Cole Younger had his face pitted with bird shot and a wound in his shoulder, and his brother Jim's jaw was partially shot away. And still the remorseless shooting continued. As Frank James ran for his horse a bullet went into his thigh. Bob Younger limped out from under the stairs and Cole, despite his wounds, hauled him up across his saddle horn. Somehow, the gang got over the bridge and headed west.

On Division Street, the shooting stopped and the dust and smoke gradually lifted. Up on the hill the church clock pointed to twenty past one. The Northfield fight was over—for the moment. The raid was the first real defeat that the James–Younger gang had ever suffered. All of them were wounded; one of them, Jim Younger, seriously. And in their desperate attempt to get away they made one more mistake—they forgot to cut the telegraph wires.

Frank James as a young man.

From his office in Northfield, the telegraph operator immediately began putting news of the raid on the wire to the entire state. By nightfall, three hundred men were on the gang's trail; the next day the number had soared to one thousand. Thick and fast came the offers of reward —one thousand dollars a man, dead or alive, from the state of Minnesota, hundreds more from the First National Bank. The railroads that had suffered in the past chipped in too. The greatest manhunt the West had ever seen was on.

That night the weather changed and rain swept over the wooded hills. It turned the roads into quagmires and washed out the gang's trail. Hiding by day and moving cautiously at night, they made their painful way west, slipping past the net that the state was trying to draw tight around them. But day by day their position grew more and more desperate. They had stolen a horse and saddle for Bob Younger, but Jim was so weak from loss of blood from his shattered jaw that he could not ride without support. Four days after the fight they were still only fifteen miles from Northfield and a posse, following their campfires and bloodstained bandages, jumped them in a ravine near Shieldsville. But once again the outlaws escaped into the timber, and they struggled on for two more days. By now they were starving, and it was in the woods near Mankato that Jesse made the terrible proposal that was to split the Jameses and the Youngers forever.

With the cold objectivity that he had learned under Quantrill, he pointed out that Jim's condition was holding them back and would lead, inevitably, to their capture. What he proposed was shooting Jim so that they could all quicken their pace. Cole is reported to have said: "Shoot him and I'll kill you," and only Frank James, coming between them, broke up the confrontation.

However it came about, the gang split up. The Youngers and Charlie Pitts, holding Jim on his horse between them, burst through the guard on the Blue Earth River bridge; Frank and Jesse, riding double on one horse, broke through a line of soldiers near Crystal Lake.

The James boys were lucky, although at first it did not seem that way. One of the soldiers fired blindly in the dark and brought their horse down, causing injuries to both brothers' right legs. Hobbling into a cornfield, they evaded pursuit, and, in the morning, stole two horses from a farmer and headed west. On the road near Sioux Falls, however, their luck changed. They met a doctor. They forced the doctor to dress their wounds, then took his clothes and disappeared. And not for three years did they trouble the West again.

The Youngers and Charlie Pitts were not so fortunate. Hiding in a stand of timber near Medalia, they sent one of their number to a nearby farm to try to buy eggs and bread. A small inquisitive boy noticed the man's ragged appearance and suspected that he was carrying a revolver under his coat. Following the man to the woods, the boy found where the gang was hiding. Within an hour he had taken the news to the sheriff and soon a posse of 150 men surrounded the timber.

With rifle and shotgun the posse pumped round after round into the woods, but even this failed to flush out the bandits. Eventually, the hunters closed in and a bitter battle took place among the trees. Step by step the Youngers retreated—it was pistol against rifle. Charlie Pitts went down, and then Cole and Jim. Finally, only Bob Younger was left

Cole Younger, Jim Younger, and Bob Younger immediately after their capture.

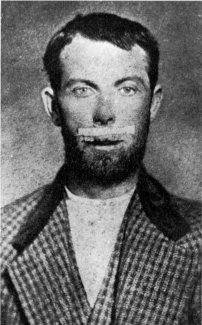

swaying among the trees, an empty gun in his left hand. "Hold your fire," he cried. "We're all down except me."

Pitts was dead, and they thought that Jim would die too. But he recovered and stood trial with his two brothers. They were charged with the murders of Heywood and Gustavson, with assault on A. E. Bunker, bank teller, and with robbery of the First National Bank of Northfield, Minnesota. They were told that under Minnesotan law they could not be hanged if they pleaded guilty. They decided that this would be their plea and they were sentenced to be confined to the State Penitentiary at Stillwater for the rest of their natural lives.

Despite their disagreement in the woods during the flight from Northfield, the Youngers did not reveal the names of their companions on the raid. The other two men, they said, were known to them as "Woods" and "Howard." And as J. B. Howard and B. J. Woodson, Jesse and Frank continued to evade the law for three more years. Then, in 1879, a train on the Chicago & Alton Railroad was held up at the Glendale station; this was the "Glendale train" of the well-known "Ballad of Jesse James." It was a holdup very similar to the one at Gad's Hill —a tiny community held captive, the railroad agent forced to flag the train down, the passengers robbed, the expressman beaten up for his keys.

The James boys were back in business, only this time there was a difference. They had gathered old companions around them, among them Dick Liddle, Bill Ryan, the Hites, Clell Miller's young brother Ed, and the Ford brothers, Bob and Charley. But only two of these men had ridden with them in the old days, and the other desperadoes were soon to play them false. Two men, Bill Ryan and Tucker Basham, were arrested after foolishly bragging about their part in the robbery. Basham turned state's evidence.

Just when the trial was about to begin Jesse struck again, this time at Winston, stopping the Rock Island Express, killing the conductor and a passenger, and getting away with ten thousand dollars.

Jesse James in the early days of his career. Note the three revolvers!

The newspapers of the day carried the story of the shooting of Jesse James in typically flamboyant style. The headline JESSE, BY JEHOVAH! appeared in the St. Joseph *Gazette,* and Bob Ford posed for pictures holding the gun he'd shot the outlaw leader with. Almost immediately, a song was written about "the dirty little coward who shot down Mr. Howard," and it became very popular.

The tide of public opinion, even in their home state, now turned against them. The Missourians had had enough of their "Bold Rovers." Ryan was sent to prison for twenty-five years. And Jesse, well and truly branded as a criminal and with the reward money piling up on his head, became the target for every two-bit gunman in the West.

More robberies followed, but time was running out. Jesse could no longer rely on his own men. Suspicious of Ed Miller, he coldly gunned him down. Murder and treachery spread among his followers. Dick Liddle killed Wood Hite, then surrendered and betrayed his brother Clarence. Bob Ford went secretly to visit the governor of Missouri. Nobody knows what deal was made between them, but whatever it was it reached fulfillment on April 3, 1882, in a little house in St. Joseph, where "Mr. and Mrs. Howard" were living with their children.

The Ford brothers went to stay with Jesse and agreed to help him rob the bank in Platte City. But at about nine o'clock in the morning, when the three of them were alone in a room and Jesse was standing on a chair dusting a picture, Bob Ford drew his pistol and shot Jesse in the head. "Murdered by a traitor and a coward whose name is not fit to appear here" runs the inscription on Jesse's gravestone. So the James–Younger gang faded into history. They had ridden longer and more successfully than any other western outlaws. But what was it all worth?

The last gun used by Jesse James.

The gang's loot has been estimated at half a million dollars. Divided among ten men over fifteen years, that doesn't amount to much more than a handsome wage. Cole Younger, in his old age, said that there was nothing like that amount of money. What they got they quickly spent. Death or imprisonment was the ultimate reward for all of them. Of the twenty-seven men who rode with the Jameses and the Youngers, seven were killed by gunfire, three were lynched, three were assassinated by their own companions in outlawry, and two committed suicide. Nine served long prison sentences, and Bob Ford was eventually killed in his own saloon in Colorado. Frank James surrendered soon after Jesse's death. At his trial he pleaded for sympathy from the southerners on the jury, and he was set free! But in poor health he drifted from job to job.

Frank James and Cole Younger are the last of the gang to be glimpsed as the outlaw years fade. Both had written their life stories, full of excuses and half-truths. Neither could settle into an ordinary life. In the end, they joined forces again and traveled with a Wild West show, exhibiting themselves to a land that had largely outgrown them.

The frontier continued to move west. As the troubles of the Civil War faded, a vast new area became known as "The Land of the Six-Shooter." It had been created by the Indian Removal Act of 1830, under which the tribes of the eastern woodlands had been forced to move to the prairies beyond Arkansas. The land they occupied was called, simply, Indian Territory. There, the Creek, Chickasaw, Cherokee, Choctaw, and Seminole had settled alongside the prairie tribes—the Osage, Kiowa, and Shawnee. Their separate nations spread over the sixty-nine thousand square miles of wooded hills and the long-grass pastures we now call Oklahoma.

It was a land without law. The only police in Indian Territory were the Indian police. Settlement by the white man was forbidden. Travel was restricted. But soon unscrupulous traders began to move in to sell guns and whisky to the Indians, and the great cattle herds from Texas cut wide swathes northward through this Indian land. The Territory became a safe refuge for the wanted man, the "Robber's Roost" of the next period of lawlessness in the history of the West.

The Outlaws of Indian Territory

After the ex-guerrillas who terrorized Missouri and Kansas at the end of the Civil War, most of the outlaws of the West were cowboys. The great days of the cattleman, the days of the big herds and big ranches, called for a drifting crew of hard riders to tend the cattle. And the exciting life of Jesse James, retold in song and story around the campfires, sounded very tempting to some of these young men. Conditions in Indian Territory, too, were very similar to those in postwar Missouri. The only law was the law of the gun. Life in the Territory was dangerous anyway, and a little rustling or holdup work would bring few extra hazards—and might just lead to riches!

Of all the gangs who copied the guerrillas perhaps the best known is the Dalton outfit. This is strange, because they were far from successful

"Holdup" by W. H. D. Koerner.

outlaws. Had it not been for the final shootout at Coffeyville in 1892, it is doubtful that they would be remembered at all.

In 1861, Louis Dalton and his family left Jackson County in Missouri and went west to Kansas. There, about eight miles north of a little frontier town called Coffeyville, he bought a farm. He had eight sons and three daughters. Life on the farm was hard, and when the old man died five of the boys left home. Frank Dalton went to Fort Smith in Arkansas, where he became a deputy; Bill Dalton went to California. Gratton

(Grat), Bob, and Emmett followed Frank and began riding for the law. It was a dangerous job and Frank was soon killed by Indian horse thieves. But the brothers were tough. They traveled all over the Territory, seeking the routes and hideouts used by the rustlers, and they gained a great knowledge of the country, which they were to put to good use in the years to come.

Bob Dalton was one of the cowboys who had grown up with the tales of the James boys ringing in his ears. At some time during those years in the Territory, he and his brothers decided to "change horses."

Thousands of cattle and horses were now being run on what was called the Cherokee Strip, and it was an easy job for the experienced rider to steal a few and slip them over the border into Kansas for a quick sale. By 1891, the Daltons were regular thieves. It was petty stealing, and like many other young criminals of their day they would have slipped into obscurity had it not been for Bob's desire to beat Jesse James!

On May 8, 1891, the northbound Santa Fe Express was flagged down at the Wharton station in Oklahoma. When the engineer cut the throttle and brought the train to a stop he found that masked men had tied up the station agent and set the signals against the train. The bandits held up the crew and robbed the express car. Just as they were leaving they saw that the station agent had struggled free of his bonds and was putting out a call for help on the telegraph line. They shot him through the window of his cabin and he collapsed, dying, over the key.

With Grat, Bob, and Emmett Dalton were four other cowboys: Bill Doolin, Blackfaced Charley Bryant (he had a distinctive powder burn on his left cheek), Bill Powers, and Dick Broadwell. The gang would have gotten clean away if they had not stopped to steal some horses during their flight. This took time, and the next day a posse seeking the horse thieves surprised the gang as they rested in some scrub. One of the posse was killed in the skirmish and the gang split up, leaving the stolen horses. Shortly after, Blackfaced Charley Bryant was caught and killed; through him, the robbery was pinned on the gang.

The railroads put out rewards, but all remained quiet until June of the following year, when another Santa Fe train was stopped by signals at

Red Rock and the Daltons climbed aboard with guns drawn. The robbery was carried out quickly and efficiently in the style of the old James–Younger raids. But the takings were small on both these raids. As yet, the Daltons were insignificant members of the outlaw league.

Then at Adair, in Kansas, they tried again. They rode into town at night and once more took the station agent prisoner. Once more they set the signals against the oncoming train. And once more, as the express panted to a halt, masked men swarmed aboard. There were armed guards on the train but they took no action until the bandits made off. Then there was indiscriminate shooting and one bystander was killed, another wounded. The Daltons got away safely, this time with seventeen thousand dollars!

By now, the gang were riding with prices on their heads—amateur outlaws, but with enough experience to make Bob Dalton boastful. He was still only twenty-two. He had proved that he could lead men. And he had stolen a considerable sum of money. What he wanted now was fame. As Emmett wrote in the book he published when he came out of prison many years later: "Bob said he could discount the James boys' work and rob two banks in one day." They decided to do this in Coffeyville.

They chose the town because they knew it well—the roads leading in and out, the alleyways near the plaza, all were familiar. Two banks, C. M. Condon's and the First National, faced each other across the square, and the Daltons had always regarded them, boyishly, as "rich" banks. To Bob Dalton it seemed a perfect setup, and he soon won over the rest of the gang to the idea.

Early in October, they left their cave hideout in the Osage Nation and traveled toward Coffeyville. A few days later they were camped on Hickory Creek, about twelve miles north of the town. That same night, they moved along familiar dirt roads and, early in the morning of October 5, stopped near a farm, where they fed their horses some corn. Shortly after nine o'clock, a farmer and his wife passed them on the road—six young men, clean shaven, well mounted, each one armed with a Winchester rifle.

A mile or two nearer the town, Bill Doolin's horse went lame. It was essential to have a good horse for the getaway, and Doolin proposed to ride back for a fine sorrel gelding they had noticed in a field, change horses, and then catch up with the others. Impatiently, Bob Dalton agreed, and the gang went on. They came into town from the west and wound their way confidently through the streets to an alley that led to a place in the plaza just below the entrance to the Condon Bank. They tethered their horses near a livery stable in the alley. Then, with amateurish haste, the Daltons each stuck on a false beard. Powers and Broadwell were unknown in the town and so disguises for them were not considered necessary. Taking their rifles from the scabbards, they all set off toward the plaza.

From the steps of his grocery store at the end of the alley, a man named McKenna saw five men stride into the square. He glanced casually at them, and so inadequate were the disguises that he recognized Bob Dalton. Three of the men turned into the Condon bank; the remaining two hurried across to the First National. Immediately suspicious, McKenna walked to where he could look through one of the windows of the bank. Inside, two people were standing with their hands raised and one of the bearded men had a leveled rifle. McKenna rushed into his store and raised the alarm. In a few seconds, men were racing from building to building, and it was not long before rifles and cartridges were being distributed from the hardware stores to anyone who would use them. It was Northfield all over again.

Inside Condon's, Grat Dalton had swept the money from the counter into an old sack. Now he ordered the cashier to open the vault. "I can't," replied the cashier. "It's on a time lock and won't be opened until 9:45." In fact, the vault had been open since 8:30 that morning, but the bandits accepted the cashier's word. "All right," said Dalton, looking at the clock on the wall, which read 9:42. "We'll wait." It was a decision that sealed the gang's fate, for in those three minutes the citizens of Coffeyville not only armed themselves but got into position.

In the First National, Bob Dalton had called the cashier, Tom Ayres, by name and ordered him to open the vault. Emmett was lining up the

After the Coffeyville raid. In this old photograph Bill Powers had been wrongly

named Tim Evans.

rest of the staff and a customer against the wall. As Bob and Ayres stepped into the vault, a burst of gunfire echoed from the south side of the plaza.

In Condon's, glass shattered and a flying splinter cut Broadwell's arm. Grat stepped quickly to the vault and pulled the door. It swung open. Calmly he began to fill the sack with the money stacked on the shelves. But now, all around the plaza, men with shotguns and rifles began to blaze away at the bank, and when Grat, Powers, and Broadwell burst through the doors carrying their sackful of money they were met by a withering crossfire.

At about the same time, Bob and Emmett shepherded their prisoners out into the plaza and prepared to follow them. But the shooting was so continuous that they changed their minds and ran for the back door instead. In the alley behind the bank a young man with a pistol tried to stop them. Without hesitation, Bob killed him. The two ran on, Emmett clutching the sackful of money, Bob with his Winchester held before him. They turned across the end of the plaza. In front of them stood two men, looking across at Condon's. Bob dropped both of them, and then, with unerring marksmanship, turned to put a bullet into Tom Ayres, who had run out of the front doors of the First National and was leveling a rifle.

Grat, Powers, and Broadwell reached the alley and raced toward the horses. Two men tried to stop them, and in a momentary tussle Grat killed one while Powers shot the pistol out of the other's hand. Bob and Emmett appeared, racing into the alley from the north side. The horses were only about sixty yards away, but it was to prove sixty yards too much. Between the horses and the bandits, on the other side of the ranch fence of the livery stable and carrying a rifle, was John Kloehr the liveryman, generally considered to be the best shot in town. And the men on the far side of the plaza, who had rushed out to help Tom Ayres, had an uninterrupted view along the alley.

As the bandits made their final dash, a fusillade of shots swept along the narrow path, splintering wood in the fences, kicking up dust between the outlaws' running feet. Kloehr calmly shot two of the horses and then turned his attention to the men. Bob Dalton saw him, but he was ejecting a shell from his Winchester when Kloehr fired. In a few terrible moments it was all over. Powers was down. Broadwell was wounded, but leaped into the saddle. Again he was struck, and a third time, but he managed to cling to the saddle horn of his bolting horse.

Emmett got into the saddle too, but seeing Bob slump down he turned and tried to pull his brother up in front of him. A blast of buckshot took him in the back. Then it was all over.

They found Broadwell dead in the grass by the roadside a little north of the town. They met a horseman on a sorrel gelding and told him excitedly about the fight. But he didn't seem interested and rode away (to reappear a little later in the story). Two hundred shots had been fired; four citizens and four bandits lay dead in the streets. The grain sacks contained over thirty thousand dollars! Bob Dalton had outdone Jesse James, certainly, but he had paid most highly for it.

For more than thirty years after the Civil War, outlaws held sway over the entire Indian Territory. They went on raids into the adjoining states of Kansas, Missouri, Arkansas, and Texas; and when the hunt became too hot they retreated into this no-man's-land where there was no white man's court and from which they could not be extradited to the states in which their crimes had been committed. As one historian puts it:

> Their savagery flaunted itself. It seemed that every white man, Negro, and half-breed who entered the country was a criminal in the state from which he had come; that the last thing on his mind at night was thievery and murder, and that they were his first thought in the morning. No American frontier ever saw leagues of robbers so desperate, any hands so red with blood. (Glenn Shirley, *The Law West of Fort Smith* [Lincoln, Neb.: University of Nebraska Press, 1968].)

Many of these desperadoes had picturesque names: Dynamite Dick, the Verdigris Kid, "Bitter Creek" Newcomb, and Jim July. But there was nothing romantic about their deeds. Ned Christie, Blue Duck, and Cher-

75

okee Bill were wanton killers who simply liked to shed blood. Bill Cook, Rufus Buck, and Sam Starr organized highly efficient gangs of looters and rustlers. And Belle Starr, who had borne Cole Younger a son back in the old days in Texas, quite deliberately carried the techniques of the guerrillas into the new territory.

In 1873, a newspaper listed a catalog of "operations of the knife and pistol"—fifteen unsolved murders committed in one little township alone! That same year, the editor of the *Western Independent,* a newspaper published at Fort Smith, Arkansas, wrote:

> We have lived in and around the Indian country since the spring of 1834 but have never known such a state of terror. Now it is murder throughout the length and breadth of Indian country . . . it is dangerous to travel alone where villains from four quarters of the United States congregate to murder, rob, and steal.

But the law was creeping slowly west from Arkansas. Soon the Indian tribes would be driven out to make way for the white farmer and rancher. Even that remote northwest corner of the Territory known as the Cherokee Strip was to be opened for settlement in the greatest "run" for free land the country had ever known. Indian Territory would soon become the state of Oklahoma. But just before that happened, in the last years of the "longriders," as they were often called, two people whom we have met before came together in a final burst of banditry.

The Doolin Gang

Bill Doolin, whose lame horse had saved him from sharing the fate of the Daltons at Coffeyville, returned to the cowboy life he had previously known, working on a big ranch, the HX Bar spread, north of Guthrie. He was a quiet and in some ways chivalrous man. But his goal was easy money, and it wasn't long before he was sounding out like-minded companions to take to the brush once more. When he had chosen ten rough, tough young men he led them north to the old cave hideout of the Daltons. And there he was joined by Bill Dalton from California!

The gang's first robbery was at Spearville, east of Dodge City; it was an easy raid that netted them eighteen thousand dollars—although they lost one man after the gang split up. Before the next foray Doolin moved camp further west, into the wild brakes of the Cimarron River. From there, they crossed into Kansas again and held up the Santa Fe Express. There was a running fight as they headed back to the Territory, and Doolin was hit in the foot. But the gang got away and added thirteen thousand dollars to their haul.

All through the summer of '93 they lay low, riding into the town of Ingalls, a few at a time, to drink and play poker in the saloons and to make plans for the bonanza that was about to come. For the West was filling up. Land-hungry pioneers were pressing for the last good farming country owned by the Indians. And eventually the government gave in. They announced that in September the Cherokee Strip would be opened for settlement. At a given signal thousands of "boomers," lined up along the borders, would race into the Strip and grab what land they could. Marshals and deputies from all over the West assembled to patrol the line and prevent "sooners" from staking out their claims before the bugle blew at noon on September 16.

Bill Doolin knew that the land rush would result in argument and gunplay. And while the lawmen were busy sorting things out, he and his gang would strike elsewhere. But as luck would have it, events turned against them. Their visits to Ingalls had become known and, under cover of the "boomers" thronging the streets, twelve deputies arrived there secretly. They gathered near a Doctor Pickering's house; this man watched the ensuing fight and left a fascinating diary about the events and his treatment of the wounded.

Bill Doolin, "Bitter Creek" Newcomb, Dynamite Dick, Tulsa Jack, and Bill Dalton were in a saloon. Arkansas Tom was asleep in a bedroom in the hotel. When "Bitter Creek" came out and mounted his horse, one of the deputies opened fire, knocking the magazine off "Bitter Creek's" gun and wounding him in the leg. In the vicious fight that followed the gang got away, taking the wounded Newcomb with them. Doolin was shot in the neck as he ran for his horse, but it did not stop him from mounting and riding off after the others. Only Arkansas Tom was captured, dismayed that the gang had left him behind. "He said he did not think they would leave him. It hurt him bad. I have never seen a man wilt so in my life," recorded Doctor Pickering. (Harry Sinclair Drago, *Outlaws on Horseback* [New York: Crown Publishers, 1964].) Three marshals lay dead and many other people were wounded by the wild gunfire —some so seriously that they died later. The gang had also been badly hit, and when the land rush started they were still in hiding, licking their wounds.

By the end of the year the Cherokee Strip had settled down. New townships sprang up, and with the towns came the law—and an organized hunt to rid the Territory of outlaws for good. Still the gang remained in hiding. Doolin married the daughter of a minister in Payne County and bought a ranch near Burden, in Kansas, where he lived under the name of William J. Barry. Whether the girl, Edith Ellsworth, realized that he was an outlaw is not known. All through the summer of '94 the peace continued . . . and then the raids began again. First the bank at Southwest City, Missouri; then the bank at Pawnee. Next, the Rock Island train at Dover, near the Daltons' old hometown of

Kingfisher. But when the gang raided the offices of the express company at Woodward, it was their last ride together.

For more and more lawmen were after them. "Bitter Creek" and Charlie Pierce were the first to go, ambushed at night near Ingalls. Then Dynamite Dick was challenged at a store near Pawnee and wounded in the gunfight that followed. He died in jail—of pneumonia! Bill Dalton was among the last to go, surrounded in a deserted ranch house and killed by a single shot as he jumped from a window.

Only Bill Doolin was left. His wife and baby son had left the ranch in Kansas to go to live at the girl's father's house in Payne County. A watch was kept on this house, and at last Bill Doolin appeared. He came at night, bearded and carrying a rifle, with a wagon that was already loaded to take his family away.

"Drop your gun and hold up your hands!" The command rang out as the outlaw led the horses down the road. In answer, Doolin wheeled and raised his rifle, and flame spat at the shadows. Both barrels of a shotgun blasted back, and the last of the "longriders" fell dead at his wife's feet.

So the Indian Territory was cleaned up and the opportunity for easy money was gone. But was it only easy money that these fierce young men were after? Henry Starr, thirty years after a lifetime of robbery and prison sentences, put it this way:

> Of course I'm interested in the money and the chance that I'll make a big haul that will make me rich, but I must admit that there's the lure of the life in the open, the rides at night, the spice of danger, the mastery over men, the pride of being able to hold a mob at bay —it tingles in my veins. I love it. It is wild adventure. I feel as I imagine the old buccaneers felt when they roved the seas with the black flag at the masthead.

The Bandit Queen

The young men weren't the only seekers after "the wild adventure." Among the outlaws of the Indian Territory, a woman reigned for several years. She was Belle Starr, "The Bandit Queen," as the newspapers were quick to name her.

She was a young girl who had been given every opportunity to grow up into a nice young woman. Her father, John Shirley, took the family to Texas in two covered wagons when Myra Belle was only fifteen. She went to school and she played the piano, no mean achievement in those frontier days. But she was a strong-willed girl with a passion for horses, and when the James and Younger boys stayed at the farm after the Liberty raid, Myra, then eighteen, was fascinated by the ex-guerrillas, particularly by handsome Cole Younger. After the outlaws left, she had a baby. The disgrace separated her from her father and she left home to enter saloon life in Dallas. A taste for fine clothes, gambling, and excitement led her, in the old-fashioned phrase, into bad company.

Fanciful tales of her exploits have filled many books; but there is no doubt that she was a personable woman, with her velvet riding habit, her beaver hat turned up rakishly and crowned with a plume, and her black mare, Venus. She took up with a young horse thief named Jim Reed and went with him into the Cherokee Nation. There she met Jim Starr and set up home with him in a one-room cabin that she called "Younger's Bend."

It is true that Belle Starr became the undisputed leader of a band of cattle and horse thieves. She planned their raids and she disposed of the loot. But it is doubtful that she ever rode with the gang on these exploits —the hard-riding, quick-shooting petticoat terror of the plains, as legends paint her.

Belle Starr.

She served nine months in Detroit prison. Her succession of "husbands" all ended up either shot or behind bars. And finally, somewhere on that lonely road to "Younger's Bend," Belle herself was murdered, probably by her last lover, Jim July.

Belle Starr's daughter, Pearl, had this gravestone carved for her mother. The horse is her favorite mare, Venus.

The frontier days were coming to an end. As the nineteenth century waned, the head of the government department that dealt with the problems of population—the superintendent of the census—published a bulletin in which he wrote:

> *Up to and including 1880 the country had a frontier of settlement, but at present, the unsettled area has been so broken into by isolated bodies of settlement that there can hardly be said to be a frontier line. In the discussion of its extent, its westward movement, etc., it cannot, therefore, any longer have a place in the census reports. (F. J. Turner and Caroline M. S. Turner,* The Frontier in American History *[1920, 1948]. Reprinted by permission of Harry Hold & Co.)*

In simple language, this historic statement meant that the frontier had swept right across the continent. There was now no line that an outlaw could cross to place himself "beyond the law."

The wilderness, the Indian Territory, the empty land to the west that had always been there, beyond the frontier, had been swamped by the great tide of settlement. The cattleman occupied the prairies with his huge herds; the farmer nibbled at the edges with plough and barbed wire. Roads and railways reached out to even the remotest corners of this vast continent.

Of course, in places, the law was stretched thin. For another decade or so the badman would roam the wild cattle towns, seek refuge in Arizona and New Mexico or on the high plains of Wyoming and Montana. He would plague the goldfields of California and the Black Hills, too. But his days were numbered.

Cowboy Desperadoes

In the spring of 1875, two carefree young cowboys rode up the trail from Texas. They were driving a herd of cattle to the Kansas railheads to sell for their employers back in Denton. Sam Bass had come west at the age of eighteen, attracted like many other young lads by the tales of life on the range and anxious to be a cowboy. For some years he worked on the ranches around Denton, in southwest Texas, spending his hard-earned money in the gambling saloons and, for a bit of fun, betting with the other young riders on the ponies.

Sam had a fast little horse that he raced against all comers. When he was fired from his job on "Dad" Egan's ranch for spending too much time racing and too little time chasing cattle, Sam took off into the Indian Territory to try his mare against the Choctaw and Cherokee ponies. On one of these trips he met another wild young cowboy in his twenties, Joel Collins, and they teamed up to go north. In Kansas, they sold the herd that their employers had entrusted to them and just kept going with the money. They planned to make their fortune in the newly opened gold-fields of the Black Hills. But the gamblers of Deadwood proved too much for them and it wasn't long before the two Texans had lost everything. There were many other young men in the rowdy gold town who were in similar trouble, and soon Sam and Joel had joined up with a few kindred spirits to rob the Deadwood stagecoach.

Their first attempt at banditry was a miserable failure. Handling the six-horse team of the Cheyenne & Black Hills stagecoach was Johnny Slaughter, one of the best drivers on the dangerous mountain division of the trail. As Sam Bass and his companions stepped out onto the road, Slaughter whipped up the horses and drove straight through the ambush.

There was the blast of a shotgun and the fearless driver pitched forward. The reins flew from his hands and he tumbled over the leather boot into the road. The guard took control of the team and the coach raced on down the trail, eventually rolling into Deadwood with bullet holes in its side panels and a wounded man on board. The agent immediately put a report on the wire:

Deadwood, March 25. Road agents attempted to rob the coach about two and a half miles from here tonight. They killed Johnny

"The Road Agent"
by Charles M. Russell.

Slaughter and wounded Mr. Iler. We start after the body now. Notify Johnny's father. (Agnes Wright Spring, *The Cheyenne & Black Hills Stage and Express Routes* [Lincoln, Neb.: University of Nebraska Press, 1948].)

And the next day a second message added:

> There were five masked men who did the deed. They were seen by two men who say they went up over the hill near the timber. Johnny dropped twenty feet. I have him in the hotel and the sheriff offers $500 reward for the murderers. (Spring, *Cheyenne & Black Hills Stage Routes*.)

The young cowboys were now wanted men. There was no going back. Three more coaches were held up after the first blundered attempt, but in each case the haul was only a few hundred dollars. Sam decided to go south and see what bigger game could be found.

As the Union Pacific Express stopped to take on water at Big Springs, Nebraska, on September 18, 1877, six masked men galloped up and took over the train. There was some delay when the messenger said that the safe was a "through" one, with a time lock that would only open when it reached its destination. The gang took an axe to the safe, but it was tough. And then, quite by chance, they opened three other boxes in the express car. They contained sixty thousand dollars in gold pieces, consigned to the Wells Fargo Bank and the National Bank of Commerce in New York. Sam Bass had found his "easy money"!

But the gang were still amateurs. Collins and a companion, riding home with their share of the loot, were challenged and killed near Fort Hays in Kansas, and some of the gold was recovered, tied up in an old pair of jeans. Another member of the gang was identified and shot by the sheriff of the little town of Mexico, Missouri. But Sam made it back to Texas. There he recruited another gang and set up camp in a long, winding ravine known as Cave Hollow. From this hideout they struck at coaches and trains, but their luck was poor and they never found more than a few thousand dollars. As railroad detectives, deputies, and rang-

Sam Bass, standing on the left; Joel Collins holds the revolver.

ers closed in, they lived like hunted animals, fighting off posses, hiding in the caves.

The end came for Sam Bass, as it did for so many badmen, through betrayal by one of his own gang. Jim Murphy, a long-standing friend, lived near Cave Hollow. At first, he and his brother, Bob, helped the outlaws, but when they were arrested and charged with harboring known criminals, Jim Murphy made a deal with the law. Released, he joined Sam Bass in Cave Hollow. And when Sam set out to rob the bank at Round Rock, Jim went along. He managed to pass a message to a telegraph office on the way, and the scene was set for Sam Bass's last ride.

It was past noon on a hot sunny day when Sam Bass led Frank Jackson, Seaborne Barnes, and Jim Murphy into Round Rock. They planned to spy out the land that evening and rob the bank the next day. Murphy slipped away, pretending to scout the town, but in reality making sure that the sheriff had gotten his message. He had. And when Sam and his companions stepped into a store, wearing their guns, the sheriff and a deputy stopped them, saying that the wearing of firearms was not permitted in the town.

Realizing that they were discovered, the outlaws drew their revolvers and shot both the sheriff and the deputy on the spot. Hearing the gunfire, a posse of Texas Rangers, who had been gathering to protect the bank, rushed to the scene. Barnes was shot down before he could mount his horse. In a hail of bullets, Sam Bass and Jackson made their escape. But the next day a farmer rode in to say that Sam was dying outside his cabin. Jackson had disappeared. For three days they questioned Sam Bass, trying to get him to name his companions. But the young cowboy refused, and at the end of those three days, on his twenty-seventh birthday, he died.

Jim Murphy didn't last a year. Despised by the people of Denton, hounded by a popular ballad that celebrated his act of betrayal, he took poison about eleven months after the shootout. So Sam Bass, the young, unsuccessful bandit—except for that one raid at Big Springs for money

Deadwood, South Dakota, 1876.

he never had the opportunity to spend—rode into legend largely on the strength of a song that, like the "Ballad of Jesse James," gave his killer a dubious epitaph.

> And so he sold out Sam and Barnes
> and left their friends to mourn,
> Oh, what a scorching Jim will get
> when Gabriel blows his horn!

The Rowdy Cow Towns

Sam Bass and Joel Collins began their careers in crime in a small town in Kansas when they decided to steal the money that they had received from the sale of those Texas longhorns. The Kansas cow towns, that string of railroad depots that began with Baxter Springs and Coffeyville and went on springing up further and further west as the tracks pushed out onto the prairie, were notorious as the settings for much gunplay. They were the towns that first gave the West its wild name: Wichita, Abilene, Caldwell, Ellsworth, Dodge City.

Primitive, often little more than one wide street of wooden buildings (many with false fronts to make them more imposing in the vast spaces around them), these towns were built for one purpose—to receive the herds coming up from Texas. There were no pavements and thousands of wheels, boots, and hooves churned the ground to knee-deep mud when it rained. In the stores that lined the street all the necessities of life could be bought: food, clothes, hardware, guns, ammunition, saddles. There were usually a smithy, stables, barber shop, bank, and restaurants. And cheek by jowl with these ordinary, respectable establishments—and frequently outnumbering them—were gambling houses, saloons, and dance halls.

Toward this speck of civilization on the plain rode the cowboy. For perhaps eleven months of the year he was a hard-working, conscientious, sober young man. He had ridden herd over several thousand head of cattle for maybe fifteen hundred miles. He'd worked long hours, day and night. He'd eaten dust in the drag and poor food when the weather had turned and put out the cook's fires. He had come through the Indian Territory and borne his share of danger bravely. And then suddenly,

91

"No Luck on the Draw" by W. H. D. Koerner.

when the cattle were safely corralled at the railhead and the trail boss had returned from town with the money, he found himself free. For a few weeks he had nothing to do and plenty to spend. Little wonder that he raced into town with a "yippee" on his lips and his revolver blazing at the sky—or at a notice that said explicitly, *"The carrying of firearms is strictly forbidden.* Signed: J. Masterson, Marshal."

Waiting for the cowboys were the gamblers, the confidence men, and assorted sharp operators. The result of such a meeting was often spectacular violence. The Wichita *Eagle* of 1874 describes the crowd in the town:

> Broad-brimmed and spurred Texans, farmers, businessmen, real-estate agents, land seekers, greasers, hungry lawyers, gamblers, women in white sunbonnets and shoes of a certain pattern, express wagons going pell-mell, prairie schooners, farm wagons, and all rushing after the almighty dollar. (Nyle H. Miller and Joseph W. Snell, *Great Gunfighters of the Kansas Cowtowns* [Lincoln, Neb.: University of Nebraska Press, 1973].)

And the account goes on:

> There was a struggle for a while over which should run the city, the hard cases or the better people. The latter got the mastery and have only kept it by holding a "tight grip." Pistols are as thick as blackberries. (Miller and Snell, *Great Gunfighters.*)

To control such a town, the "tight grip" was often held by a marshal who had been appointed chiefly because of his prowess with a gun. And the distinction between the law-abiding and the lawless was often blurred. Some marshals were apt to forget which side they were on. Billy Brooks, for example, a former stagecoach driver, became marshal of Newtown in 1872. His shadowy trail goes from Newtown to Ellsworth, where he was paid for his services as a policeman. But two years later he was hung as a horse thief!

94

Dodge City, 1880.

Varieties Saloon, Dodge City.

And there were Henry Browne and Ben Wheeler, who made up the entire police force of Caldwell in 1883. They rode down into Indian Territory looking, they said, for a murderer. A few days later, four masked men rode into the nearby town of Medicine Lodge in Kansas and went into the Medicine Valley Bank. A few moments later the town rocked to the sound of gunfire. In the pouring rain, the citizens rallied to the defense of their bank with such good effect that they were able to send this telegram to the citizens of Caldwell.

Bank robbers were Brown and Wheeler, marshal and deputy of Caldwell, and Smith and Wesley. All arrested. Tried to escape. Brown killed. Balance dead. (Miller and Snell, *Great Gunfighters.*)

Wichita, 1878.

The "balance" were Deputy Wheeler and his two cowboy companions, who were taken to the nearest tree and hanged without ceremony.

The gunfighters of the Kansas cow towns—the "Wild Bill" Hickocks, the Earps, the Mastersons—are a story apart. But some pretty notorious outlaws were also drawn to these rowdy centers . . . like Wes Hardin.

Lone Killer

An attractive young man rode up the Chisholm Trail in 1870, heading for Abilene. He was in charge of a herd of cattle from Gonzales County in Texas, and he was probably the youngest trail boss ever to make the drive. Slightly built, with mild blue eyes, he was seventeen years of age —and already a killer!

John Wesley Hardin had grown up in Texas after the Civil War. His father was a minister and he had named his son after the founder of his faith. When the boy was only fifteen, he killed a young Negro with whom he had had a boyish disagreement—this he settled in unboyish fashion by shooting him "again and again until I shot him down." His father was horrified by the deed, but because the crime of killing a freed slave would get an unsympathetic hearing in a court backed by the occupying Union troops, he urged the boy to flee. Two white men and a Negro were sent to arrest John Hardin but, helped by his Texas neighbors, he ambushed and killed all three.

Two years later he was arrested by chance. He managed to buy a gun while he was in jail and tied it under his coat. When he was being moved to face trial he shot his guard and escaped.

So far, it could be argued that he was an ordinary young man with a hasty temper, a victim of circumstances. Conditions in Texas after the war were bad. The Confederate army simply melted away before the advancing columns of the Union, and in the chaos that followed many men hit back at the "enemy." Like the James boys in Missouri, John Hardin wasn't considered that bad by his family and neighbors. . . .

Closely following Hardin up the Chisholm Trail that season was a herd of cattle driven by Mexicans. They were so close, in fact, that the young trail boss had to put two or three hands behind the drag to keep the cattle separated. At the Little Arkansas River, as Hardin's herd slowed for the crossing, the situation became even more confused and Hardin rode back to talk to the Mexican trail boss. In the row that followed a general gunfight broke out, at first between Hardin and his opposite number, then between all the rival cowboys. Six *vaqueros* were killed—five of them by John Wesley Hardin.

Abilene, the herd's destination, was one of the wildest of the Kansas cow towns. A newspaper of the time reported that during the cattle season there was a larger number of cutthroats and desperadoes in Abilene than in any other town of its size on the continent. Into this rowdy town rode Hardin's crew, preceded by the news of the fight on the riverbank. Immediately the smooth-cheeked boy who led them was nicknamed "Little Arkansaw." That first night in Abilene, Hardin got into an argument with a policeman, who backed off at the point of the Texan's gun. Within weeks he was involved in two killings: of a man he claimed had insulted Texas, and of a Mexican who had shot one of his crew. Finally came the callous deed that awoke echoes of the Harpes on the Wilderness Road.

"Little Arkansaw" was staying the night in the American House Hotel. This frail building's rooms didn't guarantee much privacy. When he heard snores coming through the wall from the next room, Hardin put two bullets through the partition. And although some people say that this killing is just another western legend, Hardin admitted to it later in his autobiography. "They tell a lot of lies about me. They say I killed six or seven men for snoring, but it isn't true. I only killed one man for snoring."

Even for Abilene the crime was too much, and Hardin got out of town at dawn on a stolen horse, never to return. But he gave the lie to those who defended him by saying that conditions in Texas had made him a killer. In the North, where those conditions didn't exist, he went from bad . . . to worse. When he got back to Texas his total killings numbered around twenty-two men.

Back at home Hardin was protected by a large number of friends. For some time he continued to dodge the law, and in 1871 he married Jane

Bower, the daughter of a local storekeeper in Gonzales County. It was a strange marriage; Jane remained true and uncomplaining, bringing up the outlaw's two children, while Hardin roamed the West, gambling.

In the town of Comanche, on his twenty-first birthday, the killing occurred that was to send John Wesley Hardin to jail at last. It was a day of horse-racing, and Hardin had won a considerable sum of money. He was celebrating in the saloon when a deputy from a nearby county walked in and saw him. He knew Hardin as a cold-blooded killer and, although he did not have a warrant for his arrest, he pulled a gun. There was a cry of "Look out!" Hardin wheeled as the deputy fired and the bullet grazed the outlaw. It was the deputy's last shot. Before he could fire again Hardin shot him in the face—his thirty-ninth victim. Since the deputy had drawn first, Hardin was allowed to walk out of town without interference.

But by now the law was determined to rid Texas of this ruthless killer, and, stopping only to collect his wife and family, Hardin fled to Florida. There, under the name of J. H. Swain, he lived for nearly two years. But detectives were on his trail. He was challenged one day near the Florida border and he shot two lawmen before fleeing into Alabama. More killings followed, usually over gambling, and then in July, 1877, he was cornered on a train by the Texas Rangers.

It was one of those strange tricks of fate whereby very ordinary things alter the course of events. As the Rangers rushed him from both ends of the car, Hardin's gun became entangled in his suspenders! He was quickly overpowered and tied up. They took him back to Texas and charged him with the killing of the deputy in Comanche. He was found guilty and sent to prison for twenty-five years. There he studied theology and law, and after serving fifteen years of his sentence was pardoned by the governor of Texas, just a year after his wife died. After his release he took his examination at the bar and with cool effrontery went to El Paso, rented an office, and hung out his notice: "Attorney at Law."

By 1894, the Southwest had become the last refuge of the outlaws. El Paso was as wild as the old Kansas cow towns had been in their time, and Hardin soon went back to gambling and drinking. He clashed with a big

John Wesley Hardin.

bearded policeman named John Selman, one of those shadowy figures sometimes on the side of the law, sometimes a rustler. Selman shot Hardin in the back as he stood at a bar playing dice. He claimed that it was a fair fight because Hardin could see him in the bar mirror!

The El Paso *Daily Herald* of August 20, 1895, reports the scene in the lurid language of the time:

> Last night between eleven and twelve o'clock San Antonio Street was thrown into an intense state of excitement by the sound of four pistol shots that occurred in the Acme Saloon. Soon the crowd surged against the door and there, right inside, lay the body of John Wesley Hardin, his blood flowing over the floor and his brains oozing out of a pistol wound that had passed through his head. Soon the facts became known that John Selman, Constable of Precinct No. 1, fired the fatal shots that had ended the career of so noted a character as Wes Hardin, by which name he is better known to all Texans. For several weeks past, trouble had been brewing, and it has often been heard on the streets that John Wesley Hardin would be the cause of some killing before he left town. (J. Marvin Hunter and Noah H. Rose, *The Album of Gunfighters,* 1951.)

This time the boot was on the other foot, and the man who had killed some forty-four men in his lifetime went down under the gun himself.

A nearly completed manuscript was found among his possessions, and in 1896 his son published the autobiography. Copies of the original are quite scarce, because it was withdrawn only a few days after publication.

Wes Hardin was typical of the solitary killers who roamed the West during the cowboy decades. Mostly southerners, they came from ordinary, hard-working families and seemed to have no excuse for their evil life. They broke from home at an early age and set off into a land that was still raw and rough. And if they felt a sudden impulse to violence when someone got in their way, or for some quite trivial reason, there was nothing to restrain them—no settled community to voice disapproval, no routine of normal behavior by which their misdeeds could be judged.

Bill Longley was one such loner—a cowboy, farmhand, and gambler who moved from the Indian Territory to the Black Hills and back again to Texas, taking violence with him wherever he went and ending up on the gallows at the age of twenty-seven, the unrepentant killer of thirty-two men.

Clay Allison, too—discharged from the Confederate army with a medical record of a wound that may have had some effect on his wild behavior—became in turn a cowpuncher, a trail hand, and, finally, a rancher. But despite his prosperity he was a quick-tempered alcoholic who left a trail of dead men across the range until one day, hauling supplies home to his ranch from the little town of Pecos, he fell from the wagon and broke his neck.

Farther west still, an Indian ex-scout, the Apache Kid, began a career of murder simply by obeying tribal custom and killing the killer of his father. When the white man's law said that he should not take retribution into his own hands, he embarked on a one-man reign of terror throughout Arizona and ran up a total of killings that has not been fully reckoned to this day.

The ranchers, too, were moving west. In the southeastern corner of

Clay Allison.   Bill Longley.   The Apache Kid.

New Mexico, all along the Pecos River, there was fine grazing land unreached as yet by the railroad, and untouched by the farmer with his barbed wire. This free range offered the promise of great wealth, not only to the cattlemen who could hold it but to the big business interests now turning to the West. The cattle industry had assumed huge proportions, and powerful groups of men began to struggle for its control. They fought not only for the rich grazing land on which to run the vast herds, but for all the commerce that went with it, and, eventually, for political control of the state. Into this last lawless refuge, fleeing west from the Texas Rangers and ready to hire out their guns to the highest bidder, rode the last of the badmen. They rode into the Lincoln County War.

Lincoln County in the 1870s covered twenty-seven thousand square miles of grass, most of it in the public domain (free land, open to anyone for grazing). Trouble had been simmering in the county for many years —it was a complicated story of deceit and corruption. The first cattleman to move into the area from Texas was John Chisum, with a vast herd numbering ten thousand head. He spread them along both banks of the never-failing Pecos River for about 150 miles south of Fort Sumner, and then, according to custom, claimed the range as his own for as far back as a man could ride in a day. Next he began to buy up the herds of the smaller ranchers and add them to his cattle kingdom. The small men resented Chisum's growing domination of the Pecos valley, believing that he was out to drive them from their homes. Rustlers moved in to take advantage of the situation and accusations began to fly thick and fast between Chisum and the other ranchers.

In 1875 an Irishman, an ex-major named Lawrence Murphy, was running a mighty profitable business in the county seat, Lincoln. He owned a flour mill, a saloon, a hotel, and a huge store that he called "The Big House." Through his old army friends he had obtained contracts to supply Fort Stanton and the Apache Indian reservation with beef. And, although he had only a small ranch, he seemed able to sell them an amazing number of steers each year. The cattle were not all coming from the small Murphy spread, of course. With his partners, J. J. Dolan and

J. H. Riley, the astute major was buying beef at five dollars a head—not being too particular whose brand the animals carried—and selling them at fifteen or twenty dollars a head. A handsome profit! There were other shady deals, too, like the overestimation of Indians on the reservation —"The Big House" getting paid for supplying 1,100 Indians a week when in fact there were only 400—and wagonloads of stores ostensibly bought by the government that simply disappeared. Pretty soon, through his friends in the capital at Santa Fe, Major Murphy and "The

"The Rustlers" by W. H. D. Koerner.

House" ruled the roost throughout the county, with lawmen and U.S. troops almost at beck and call.

Chisum, of course, resented this. He didn't see why middlemen, who weren't cattlemen anyway, should reap the profits on beef supplied to the army. He wanted to sell his cattle direct to Fort Stanton himself; and he wanted to put a stop to the rustling. At last, Chisum's men caught a group of rustlers in the act and hauled them off to town, where warrants were sworn out against them. Major Murphy tried to get a young lawyer named Alexander McSween, who had just arrived in town from Kansas with his bride, to defend the rustlers. But McSween refused; the men were clearly guilty, he said, and he couldn't defend them with a clear conscience.

To complicate matters, a young Englishman named John Tunstall arrived in Lincoln County at around this time. His father, a rich business-man in London, had sent him over to look at the prospects of raising sheep in New Mexico. Tunstall bought a ranch on the Feliz River and became friendly with Chisum and McSween. It wasn't long before the three men went into partnership. They opened a store in Lincoln, and then a bank. John Chisum's name appeared as that of the president of the bank. All this threatened Major Murphy's monopoly in the county, and to the citizens of Lincoln it was obvious that before long there would be a showdown. Into this explosive situation, one autumn day in 1877, rode a lad of seventeen, slightly built, blue-eyed, and with an engaging grin. His name was McCarty or Bonney or sometimes Antrim . . . or just "the Kid."

Fast Action

That fast draw, the ability of a gunman—marshal or outlaw—to get his pistol out of its holster and into his hand ready for firing, is a trick you have seen hundreds of times on television and the screen. Modern marksmen and entertainers undoubtedly *can* perfect the fast draw with practice. But was it really used by the badmen of the Old West?

First of all, you must remember Sam Colt's "Equalizer," described on pages 37–41. The cumbersome "cap and ball" pistols were temperamental. Percussion caps could be knocked off, paper cartridges became damp. So Quantrill's guerrillas, for example, carried several revolvers to make sure that they would be able to get off an effective number of shots before the time came to reload. Jesse James and the Youngers were skilled marksmen, but the fast draw was something they knew nothing about. It was not until the all-metal cartridge came into general use and the foolproof "Peacemaker" made its appearance that the act of drawing a gun quickly from its holster could be attempted.

Then, perhaps, a cutaway holster would be worn low on the thigh. The gunman would drop his hand onto the protruding butt of the "Peacemaker," his thumb falling on the hammer and his finger slipping into the trigger guard exposed by the "cutaway." An upward pull and the draw had commenced (see Figure 1). As the gun came out of the holster and the barrel began to rise toward its target, the thumb drew the hammer back, cocking the gun. Then, as the barrel came level, everything was ready. A touch on the trigger was all that was needed to send the bullet speeding in the desired direction (see Figure 2).

To speed up his shooting, the gunman could "fan" his gun. That is, instead of using his thumb to cock the gun as he pulled it from the holster, he merely slipped his finger around the trigger and pulled it

107

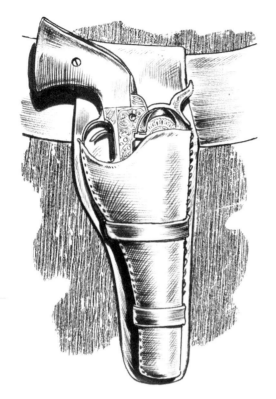

Western "cutaway" holster.

The cross draw.

Figure 1

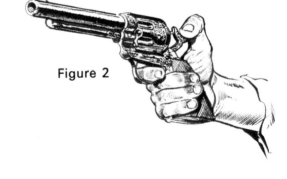

Figure 2

tight as he leveled the gun. Simultaneously he brought his left hand up, fingers outstretched and palm held vertical. Sweeping the hand across the gun the bottom edge of his palm would catch the hammer and pull it back, releasing it as the hand moved on so that it fell and fired the gun. This fanning movement could be repeated more quickly than the separate movements of cocking the gun and pulling the trigger, thus sending off several shots in rapid succession (see Figure 3). But it was not a very accurate method of shooting and only gained time with the single-action gun. When the double-action Colts came in there was no need to fan.

However fast a man could pull a gun from his holster, accurate shooting was the trademark of the professional. Many a gunfight began with pistols already drawn before the gunman stalked his victim, and all sorts of tricks were resorted to in order to "get the drop" on the opposition.

A derringer, a small, single-shot pistol, could be carried secretly up the sleeve. Clipped into a spring attached to the wrist by a leather strap, it could be palmed quietly by bending the hand back and pulling gently on the butt. Or it could be shot into the hand by a rapid downward jerk of the arm (see Figure 4).

Another trick was "Curly Bill's spin," said to have originated in Tombstone, Arizona, when Curly Bill Graham was ordered by the town marshal to "Hand over that gun—butt first!" He presented the Colt as ordered, but kept his forefinger extended through the trigger guard. As the marshal reached for the weapon, Curly Bill jerked his hand slightly and the perfectly balanced weapon spun around. The butt slapped into

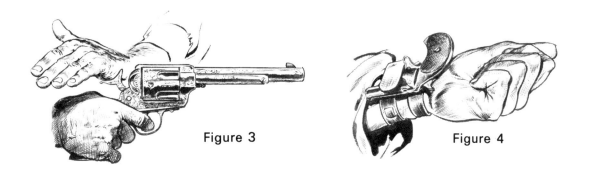

Figure 3   Figure 4

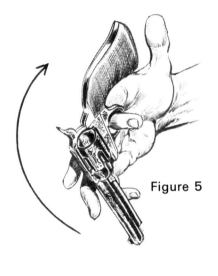

Figure 5

Figure 6

the gunman's palm and the astonished marshal found himself looking down the barrel (see Figure 5).

The shoulder holster was an almost completely cutaway design; it was worn strapped high under the left armpit. The muzzle of the pistol rested in a leather cup at the bottom of the holster and the gun was held in place by a spring. An open coat or vest covered the whole thing. To draw, the gunman had only to slip his hand under his coat and pull the gun from the clip (see Figure 6). There were many other styles of shoulder holster, all designed to keep the weapon hidden.

These are some of the tricks of the gunfighter's trade. But the fast draw of the films should be taken with a large pinch of salt. A gun in the hand or hidden under a coat, a shot from ambush, a shot in the back— these are more likely to have been the methods of the men we are talking about in this book. Badmen had few scruples and they certainly did not follow a "code of the West."

Billy the Kid

Probably over five hundred books have been written about Billy the Kid. They present an amazing picture of a boy who was adept at cards at the age of eight . . . who killed a man who insulted his mother when he was only twelve . . . who rode with other young desperadoes and carelessly dispatched countless Mexicans and Indians—a bold, handsome fellow who dressed neatly, was exceedingly polite to young and old alike, and who laughed a lot. Hardly any of it is true, except perhaps that he laughed a lot. Pat Garrett, who tended bar in Fort Sumner one summer and knew the Kid as a customer—that same Pat Garrett who was later elected sheriff and killed the Kid—said, "Those who knew him well will tell you that in his most savage and dangerous moods his face always wore a smile. He ate and laughed, drank and laughed, rode and laughed, talked and laughed, fought and laughed—and killed and laughed!" (Paul Trachtman, *The Gunfighters* [New York: Time-Life Books, 1974].)

The boy was born in New York around 1860; the date is not definite. He was the second son of Catherine McCarty Bonney and his father was Patrick Henry McCarty or William Bonney—the records are that vague. His father died sometime near the end of the Civil War and Catherine took her boys to Indiana. There she met and married William Antrim, a big, bearded man who was sometimes a carpenter, sometimes a bartender, but at heart a miner. Antrim took his family to Silver City, New Mexico, and Mrs. Antrim started a boardinghouse. Billy went to school and was no more trouble than any other boy in a frontier town. When his mother died, Billy worked for his board in the hotel. And when he was fifteen he had his first brush with the law. Some clothes were stolen from a Chinese laundry for a prank; but Billy's companion in the game disappeared and Billy was left holding the bag. Arrested as Henry

McCarty, he escaped from jail by worming his way up the chimney.

In the next few years, Kid Antrim worked as a ranch hand and a sheepherder in southeastern Arizona. Then he turned up as a teamster on the wood train out of Camp Grant—a smooth-faced boy wearing a gun to let people know he was a man. At Camp Grant he got into an argument with a man named "Windy" Cahill, and in a half-serious, half-amusing wrestling match Cahill threw the boy to the ground. Billy was wearing his gun and now he used it. Cahill died the next day and the Kid was put into the camp guardhouse. A few nights later he broke out, stole a horse, and headed for Silver City, where he stayed in hiding for a few days before leaving for the Rio Grande valley.

The next time he was seen he was walking barefoot and was near exhaustion. Looking for work around Mesilla he had been jumped by Indians, who had robbed him and taken his horse. He staggered into the ranch of a man named Heiskell Jones, who took him in and befriended him while his raw feet healed. The Kid stayed at the ranch for a while, helping Mrs. Jones. Throughout his short life he seems to have found the need to attach himself to somebody, to stay around people and places he knew. It was a loyalty that was to cost him dearly.

Heiskell Jones lent him a horse and one day in September he rode up the Pecos, past the Chisum ranch, and into Lincoln. He took a job on Tunstall's ranch on the Rio Feliz. The legends say that a bond of friendship sprang up between the drifting young cowboy and the cultured Englishman, but Tunstall makes no mention of Billy in his diary. The Kid was to demonstrate a newfound loyalty in the months to come, certainly; but whether it was because of his fair-minded employer or because he found himself leading men for the first time will never be known.

"The House" now decided to move against the threat to their monopoly. They hatched a scheme of accusing McSween and Tunstall of an old debt, and claimed a herd of Tunstall's horses as payment. Tunstall refused to hand them over. Sheriff William Brady—who had served in the army under Major Murphy—mustered a posse and sent it to collect the animals. Hearing that twenty-five men were riding against him, Tunstall said that he would argue the case in the courts and not with a gang

William Bonney, alias the Kid, alias Antrim.

of thugs. Rounding up a few of the horses and accompanied by ranch foreman Dick Brewer, the Kid, and several cowhands, he set off for Lincoln to prove that the animals were indisputably his own. In spite of warnings that the posse contained several known criminals, he could not believe that it spelled danger to him personally.

When the posse caught up with the little party, Tunstall turned back to talk, while Brewer and the Kid held the horses a little way off. The argument proceeded with the mounted posse milling around the lone Englishman. Suddenly, without the slightest provocation, two men drew their revolvers and shot Tunstall in the head. Within minutes he was dead and the posse were riding away. It was a cold-blooded, unjustified killing and whether or not the Kid rode down and swore vengeance over Tunstall's body, as the stories say, he now threw himself wholeheartedly into the fight against "The House" and its allies.

Lincoln County immediately took sides: those who had suffered at the hands of "The House" threw in their lot with McSween; those who thought that Chisum was out to drive them off the range joined Major Murphy. War had been declared.

Tunstall's friends swore later that the sheriff's posse "was composed of the worst murderers and thieves of southern New Mexico." Warrants were taken out against the killers, and Billy was among the citizens who tried to move against Bill Morton, one of the men who had fired at Tunstall. But Major Murphy was a good friend of the governor of the state and he persuaded him to fire the justice of the peace who had issued the warrants. The warrants were then declared useless and Billy was thrown into jail for three days for interfering with one of the deputies. His rifle was taken from him.

When he was released he joined Dick Brewer, Tunstall's foreman, and with a group of citizens formed a party of "Regulators." They set off to hunt for Tunstall's killers. They trailed Bill Morton and a man named Frank Baker to the Rio Panesco valley and captured them after a long fight. The Kid was for killing the men outright, but the Regulators were still trying to act legally and they set off with their prisoners for the town. On the third day of their journey, when the party were strung out down the Rio Bonito canyon, the Kid shot the unarmed men. Dead in the canyon, too, lay a deputy who had tried to protect them.

A few weeks later, in April, came the next savage outburst. As Sheriff Brady and three men walked past Tunstall's old store in the town, a volley of shots rang out and Brady and a deputy fell dead. The other men fled. Before the noise of the shooting had even faded, Billy came out of the store and stood over the body of the man who had sent that first posse after Tunstall. He picked up the sheriff's rifle and walked away.

These killings swung the town against the Regulators, just as Tunstall's death had aroused hatred for "The House." Both sides were now gathering men of dubious reputation about them. "Lincoln County," said Isaac Ellis, a merchant of the town at the time, "is today totally in the hands of thieves, and all law-and-order-loving citizens are forced to seek elsewhere the protection and safety of their and their families' lives." (*The True Story of Billy the Kid*, Panther Books, 1959.) A new sheriff was appointed through Murphy's influence, a man named George Peppin, one of Brady's former deputies. But Dick Brewer still rode as a "policeman" with the Regulators. Things were hotting up for the final battle. At a place called Blazer's Mill, Dick Brewer and thirteen of the Regulators—the Kid, Charlie Bowdre, Tom O'Folliard, George and Frank Coe, John Middleton, and Henry Brown among them—cornered an old buffalo hunter named "Buckshot" Roberts who had been in the posse that had killed Tunstall. Roberts had been wounded many years before and a load of buckshot in his right shoulder prevented him from raising his rifle. He did his shooting from the hip, and with such deadly accuracy that his first shots cut down Bowdre and took off George Coe's thumb. Next he put Middleton out of the fight with a bullet through the lung. Bowdre, however, had wounded the old hunter in the chest, and the others closed in. Roberts was tough. He kept firing until his gun was empty; then, when the Kid reached him, he jabbed the gun bayonet-style into his stomach. As the Kid doubled up Roberts staggered into the mill where they had found him. He pulled a Springfield rifle down from the wall and grabbed some cartridges. Then he dragged a mattress from a cot and threw it across the half-open door. Loading the gun, he lay down and waited. When Brewer emerged from a woodpile about a hundred yards away, Roberts steadied the Springfield and shot him through the left eye.

The Regulators retreated, leaving Brewer dead. The old buffalo hunter was not long in following him, and they were buried side by side the next day.

There were more skirmishes between Chisum's cowboys and the Murphy men. And then, in the middle of July, the fighting erupted into a pitched battle in the middle of Lincoln. The Kid, who had taken Brewer's place, led his gang into Lincoln one hot summer afternoon. They fortified themselves in McSween's adobe house in the center of the town. McSween, a lawyer to the last, refused to take up arms; but he and his wife accepted the presence of the men and welcomed the next arrivals. These were a group of Mexicans from the villages below the town who had long resented Major Murphy's ruthless trading methods and high prices. About twenty-five armed men were in the house when night fell. In the darkness, Sheriff Peppin and a large force of men surrounded the sleeping town. They closed in on the house and at dawn called upon the Regulators to surrender. There was no response, but as the morning wore on desultory shooting broke out and continued throughout the day. There were no casualties, however.

The next night, Peppin positioned his men at vantage points around the house, two of them on high rocks overlooking McSween's patio. In the morning firing started again and, with an extraordinary display of marksmanship, an old Mexican in the house, Fernando Herrara, picked off the men on the mountaintop with a Sharps buffalo gun. Throughout the day the besiegers poured shot after shot into the house, but the thick adobe walls took the battering well and the defenders kept clear of the windows. At one stage of the fight, Peppin's guns found a piano in a front room and each time it was hit wild discords rang out amidst the gunfire. During a lull in the shooting, Mrs. McSween and two other women in the house were persuaded to leave, and a brief truce held while they did so.

That evening, Colonel Dudley of Fort Stanton came riding in with two companies of Negro cavalry. By this time, fighting had broken out in other parts of the town as the Mexican population tried to help McSween. Although Dudley had no orders to use his troops to quell a civil disturbance, he was very much on the side of Major Murphy. When one of his messengers came under fire from the besieged house, he used the incident as an excuse to trail a howitzer through the town and position it about thirty yards from the home of a prominent Mexican citizen. He then said that if they raised one finger to help McSween and his men he'd blow the house apart. So the gang was now cut off from all aid, and on the fifth day of the fight Peppin's men managed to get close enough to pile brushwood against the adobe walls and set fire to it.

Slowly the flames crept through the wooden parts of the building, eating up the floors, burning the furniture. Choking with the smoke, the defenders retreated from room to room. McSween was now depressed and very pessimistic about the outcome of the fight—the violent action was not of his choosing—but the Kid had no intention of giving in. He shot one Mexican who tried to surrender; and when a messenger got as far as the gate with a note demanding surrender, he killed him, too.

As night fell, it was obvious that the gang must surrender or escape. The Kid split them into two groups and, on a given signal, they burst out. The Kid, Bowdre, O'Folliard, a Mexican, and a young man named Morris, who was studying law with McSween, reached the wall on the east side of the house. There Morris went down, but the others scrambled over and reached Tunstall's store. In a hail of bullets they ran for the Bonito River bottom and got away to safety in the darkness.

The second group, mainly Mexicans, tried to force a passage toward a gate behind the house but were turned back. They tried again; again gunfire stopped them. Then a voice was heard asking if their surrender would be accepted. It was thought to be McSween. Robert Beckwith shouted back that he was a deputy and would accept the surrender. As he stepped forward two Mexicans shot him.

A roar of gunfire broke out like a roar of rage, and when it had stopped McSween lay dead across Beckwith's body. Three Mexicans were sprawled in the gateway. Gunsmoke and smoke from the burning house drifted across the town as Tunstall's store was looted. But the Lincoln County War was finished.

Although Peppin's men had won the day—McSween dead, Billy the Kid on the run, and Chisum losing interest in the whole affair—order did not return to Lincoln County for a long time. The Regulators scattered and set up bands of their own to murder and steal. Rustlers grew bolder and ranchers died defending their herds. So bad did things become that Sheriff George Peppin, who, to his credit, was trying to do his job conscientiously, reported that he could not gather the taxes and dared not visit the county seat without fifteen or twenty men at his back. Settlers began to leave the district; and, alarmed at the continuing disorder, the government appointed a new governor—General Lew Wallace, the author of *Ben Hur*.

One of the first things Wallace did was to proclaim amnesty. This meant that all citizens who had taken up arms in the recent troubles could return to their peaceful occupations and no action would be taken against them. But there was one condition—no amnesty would be granted to men who already had a warrant sworn against them. And as Billy the Kid was still wanted for the murder of Sheriff Brady, he remained an outlaw with a price on his head. Five hundred dollars, the governor offered, to any man who would deliver William Bonney, alias the Kid, to any sheriff's office in New Mexico. So weary were the citizens of the constant outlawry that they raised the price to one thousand five hundred dollars!

But still the Kid remained free. Unable to tear himself away from familiar people and familiar places, he gathered a gang around him—Charlie Bowdre, Tom O'Folliard, and a few of the old lawless Regulators—and began to rustle John Chisum's cattle and to steal horses from the Indian reservation. In between these activities, he hung around Fort Sumner, daring anyone to arrest him and gambling and drinking. From time to time the old rivalry of the range flared up. A lawyer, Houston Chapman, was employed by Mrs. McSween to look after her husband's affairs. James Dolan, who had taken over Tunstall's old ranch, and one of his cowboys, named Campbell, met the lawyer in the street. Campbell was drunk and ordered Chapman to dance on the sidewalk. The lawyer refused, and the cowboy shot him while Billy and his gang looked on.

At last Wallace saw that there would be no peace in Lincoln County until the Kid was behind bars. After an exchange of messages, the novel-writing governor and the young outlaw met secretly. Wallace offered the Kid a pardon if he would submit to arrest and turn state's evidence on Chapman's murderer. Billy surrendered, but after some days in the Lincoln jail he became suspicious of Wallace's promise, slipped the handcuffs from his slim wrists, and walked away.

The raiding started all over again. The Kid and other desperadoes terrorized all of southeastern New Mexico and struck across the border at the ranches in the Texas Panhandle. At last, Chisum and the leading citizens of the county got together. In November of 1880, Pat Garrett was elected sheriff with one top-priority task—to get the Kid!

One of the most famous manhunts of the West now began. The feud between the Murphy and McSween factions was all but dead. Garrett had the support of all the citizens in his efforts to restore law and order. Tall, soft-spoken, determined, he went methodically about his task. He had known the Kid for a long time and, backed by his understanding of Billy's habits and personality, he laid his traps. The first success came when he set a constant watch on the old hospital at Fort Sumner. There Charlie Bowdre's Mexican wife lived and there the gang sometimes visited. When they rode into town one night they were challenged. Tom O'Folliard was killed, but Billy and the rest got away.

From camp to camp the posse followed their trail, picking up scraps of information from herders and ranchers, gradually closing in on the gang. At last they traced them to an old stone house near Stinking Springs. Surrounding the place at night, they waited. When a man came out, slightly built like the Kid, seven rifles flamed in the dim light. It was Charlie Bowdre.

All the next day the posse kept the gang pinned down in the house, killing their horses and rendering escape impossible. Then, when there was no food or water left in the house, Garrett's men lit a fire and began

to fry some food within smelling range of the outlaws. After a time the gang surrendered. Clapping leg irons on the prisoners, the sheriff hauled them to Fort Sumner in a wagon.

In Mesilla, in March, 1881, the Kid faced trial for the murder of Sheriff Brady and was sentenced to death.

Billy now felt that he had been abandoned by all his old friends and was being made the scapegoat for all of the Lincoln County War killings. He sent a letter to the governor accusing him of going back on his promise. Wallace's answer was to publish all the correspondence between them. It showed clearly that Billy had walked away from any possible pardon when he'd refused to testify about Chapman's death. The governor was not giving the Kid another chance.

The sentence called for Billy the Kid to be hung at Lincoln, and Pat Garrett appointed two deputies to take the Kid there. The men were Bob Olinger, a man who had fought for "The House" and who now threatened to kill the Kid if he made the slightest move to escape, and a kindlier man named J. W. Bell. In Lincoln, the Kid was kept in "The Big House," the old Murphy store, which had been converted into the county courthouse. He was locked in an upstairs room and shackled both hand and foot.

On April 28, just fifteen days before he was due to be hanged, he made the usual request to go to the lavatory, which was outside the main building. Bell, who was on duty, took him down the steep stairs and across to the privy. When the Kid came out again the deputy saw that he had a gun in his hand—the story is that a Mexican friend of the Kid's had hidden it there some time before. Bell jumped for the stairs but he was too late. The Kid's shot tore into him and he staggered into the yard, dying.

Scrambling up the stairs as quickly as he could in leg irons, the Kid broke into Garrett's office. Bob Olinger, who had heard the shot, came running to the scene. Old Geiss, the caretaker, had seen Bell die, and he called a warning. But Olinger was already in the yard. "Hello, Bob,"

"The Lynchers" by W. H. D. Koerner.

"Pat Garrett Brings in Billy the Kid" by J. N. Marchand.

said the Kid cheerfully. Olinger looked up at Garrett's window and saw that the Kid held a shotgun in his manacled hands. It was the last thing he saw, for the Kid pulled the trigger and a blast of buckshot hurled the deputy to the ground.

The Kid came out onto the balcony, threw the gun down on top of Olinger's body, and then went to help himself to Garrett's Winchester and six-guns. He called to Geiss to bring a file and got the caretaker to pry off his irons. He appeared to be in no hurry and called to people passing in the street. Eventually, he mounted up and rode away. Nobody tried to stop him.

Methodically, Garrett went back to work. And still the Kid stayed around instead of riding clear out of the state! Garrett kept relentlessly on his trail, picking up a clue here and there, never far behind. For two months the hunt went on and then, incredibly, it led back to Fort Sumner. Garrett felt that the end was near. It was night when the posse

To the sheriff of Lincoln County, New Mexico—
Greetings:

At the March term, A.D. 1881, of the District Court for the Third Judicial District of New Mexico, held at La Mesilla in the county of Dona Ana, William Bonney, alias Kid, alias William Antrim, was duly convicted of the crime of Murder in the First Degree; and on the fifteenth day of said term, the same being the thirteenth day of April, A.D. 1881, the judgment and sentence of said court were pronounced against the said William Bonney, alias Kid, alias William Antrim, upon said conviction according to law; whereby the said William Bonney, alias Kid, alias William Antrim, was adjudged and sentenced to be hanged by the neck until dead by the Sheriff of the said county of Lincoln, within said county.

Therefore, you, the Sheriff of the said county of Lincoln, are hereby commanded that, on Friday, the thirteenth day of May, A.D. 1881, pursuant to the said judgment and sentence of the said court, you take the said William Bonney, alias Kid, alias William Antrim, from the county jail of the county of Lincoln where he is now confined, to some safe and convenient place within the said county, and there, between the hours of ten o'clock A.M. and three o'clock P.M. of said day, you hang the said William Bonney, alias Kid, alias William Antrim, by the neck until he is dead. And make due return of your acts hereunder.

Done at Santa Fe in the Territory of New Mexico, this 30th day of April, A.D. 1881.
Witness my hand and the great seal of the Territory.

Lew Wallace
Governor, New Mexico

By the Governor
W. G. Ritch
Secretary
N.M.

Billy the Kid's death warrant.

approached the town, and he told his deputies to dismount and leave the horses on the outskirts. They went the last stretch on foot, quietly, in the dark. Garrett led the way to the old Officer's Row, where he knew a man named Maxwell who had been a friend of the Kid. It was past midnight. Maxwell was in bed. Quietly Garrett moved along the front of the building and slipped into Maxwell's room. Sitting on the bed, he whispered his questions.

At that moment a man came along the verandah in his stocking feet. It seemed as if he had a knife in his hand and was making for the kitchen. Something caught this padding figure's attention. Perhaps he saw the motionless, waiting deputies. Perhaps he just *felt* that all was not well. He ducked into Maxwell's bedroom. "Pete, who are they?" It was a young voice. Garrett cocked his pistol. In the blackness the click echoed around the room. "*¿Quién es? ¿Quién es?*" ("Who's that? Who's that?") The slight figure backed toward the doorway. Garrett fired twice.

When the noise had died away and the deputies' booted feet clattered on the boards, they brought a light. He was curled up on the floor. Some reports say that he had a knife in his hand. Garrett's story says that he had a gun, although it had not been fired. Either way, the Kid was dead.

The End.

Afterword

> I'll sing you a true song of Billy the Kid,
> I'll sing of the desperate deeds that he did.

Just what were those desperate deeds?

By the time he died at the age of twenty-one, William Bonney had killed nine men; of these, at least one was shot without warning from ambush, one was of his own company, and one was unarmed.

He had stolen a lot of cattle, not only from John Chisum's herds in the range war, but from ranchers all over the territory.

He had stolen horses from the Indians on the reservations.

He had used his guns and his gang to create such a state of terror in the country that many settlers were forced to leave, taking their frightened wives and children with them.

Hardly deeds worth preserving in song, you might think. But many songs, stories, and films present the badmen of the West as romantic figures.

> Charlie Quantrill 'O, Charlie Quantrill 'O,
> Bold, gay, and daring stood old Charlie
> Quantrill 'O.

A hundred and forty-two inhabitants of Lawrence would sing otherwise, if they could.

> Oh, Jesse was a man and a friend to the poor,
> He would never see a man suffer pain.

What about the Union soldiers on the train at Centralia? What about

George Wymore, the student on his way to classes on the day of the Liberty raid?

> Sam Bass came down to Texas, a cowboy for to be,
> A kinder-hearted feller you seldom ever see.

What would Johnny Slaughter, the driver of the Cheyenne & Black Hills stagecoach, have to say about that?

No, in spite of the legends these men, without exception, were evil men. And if the excuse is offered that conditions in the West at the time drove them to outlawry, then remember that for every badman there were a thousand pioneers who overcame those conditions and lived an honest life.

The Harpes, Quantrill, the Jameses, the Youngers—this book has told the stories of only some of the badmen of the West. You probably know of many more, like Joaquin Murietta of old California, the Plummer gang, and Butch Cassidy and the Wild Bunch. But I have selected the men in this book because I think that their stories reflect the slow procession of history across the continent. Even as they were performing their evil deeds, civilization was coming slowly but surely to the Wild West.

And throughout these tales, unless it has been absolutely necessary, I have said very little about the men who fought for law and order. This is not because their part is not exciting; on the contrary, they deserve a book to themselves. But in portraying the badmen of the Old West I have preferred to use the terms "the law" or "the sheriff" rather than have these brave men parade as minor characters in the drama.

This book belongs to the badmen; and that's just what they were, whether they had only a moment's limelight, like Joe Brown on the Shasta road, or whether they are still remembered, like Billy the Kid. *Bad* men; no more, no less than that.

Index

Riverside
County
LIBRARY SYSTEM

www.rivlib.net